a drop
of rain

D0062436

a drop of rain

Heather Kirk

Napoleon Publishing

Text © 2004 Heather Kirk

Cover art: June Lawrason

Published by Napoleon Publishing
Toronto, Ontario, Canada

Le Conseil des Arts du Canada depuis 1957 | The Canada Council for the Arts since 1957

Napoleon Publishing acknowledges the support of the Canada Council for our publishing programme.

Printed in Canada

08 07 06 05 04   5 4 3 2 1

Kirk, Heather, date-
    A drop of rain / Heather Kirk.

ISBN 1-894917-10-3

    I. Title.

PS8571.I636D76 2004   jC813'.6   C2004-900010-1

For Wanda

Human life is not just an abstraction; human life is the concrete reality of a being that lives, that acts, that grows and develops; human life is the concrete reality of a being that is capable of love, and of service to humanity.

-Pope John Paul II

1999

Week One

Naomi

Saturday, September 11, 1999

Do I Have AIDS?

Don't worry, Mrs. Henderson, I probably don't. But I *might*. I'd better explain.

My mother's older sister, Hanna, "adopted" two young men who had AIDS. Aunt Hanna took care of these men as they were dying. Now Hanna is dying too, and she is staying at our house. She has no one else to take care of her.

Hanna has cancer. But she thinks she might have AIDS too, and the test results are not back yet. My mother and the head nurse told me I won't get AIDS from living in the same house as Hanna, as long as everyone is careful. But how careful is careful? I saw the head nurse's report today. It says the nurses have to use "universal precautions" with Hanna.

If the nurses have to wear gloves, maybe Mom and I should too.

I am very angry with Hanna. Why did she get into so

much trouble? Aren't adults supposed to know better? Hanna has ruined my life. And I don't just mean that she might have given me AIDS. I have other problems too, but I don't feel like writing about them now.

*   *   *

Seven minutes down and fifty-three to go. Have to keep writing for "at least one hour", you said. "One thousand words minimum. Once a week. Until the eve of the new millenium. A time capsule. Automatic writing. Let your thoughts flow. Get in touch with your feelings. One half of your final mark."

I guess I can do this. My mother has started a journal too. A nurse said that she could do this to "help her sort out her feelings". Is that the same as "getting in touch"? Mom is depressed because Hanna is dying.

What am I going to write about?

*   *   *

You said to introduce ourselves, so here goes.

Mom says I was named after a girl in a poem by Mr. Irving Layton, a famous Canadian poet. The poem is called "Song for Naomi." Mr. Layton wrote it for his daughter. A copy of it is framed and hanging in the room where I am right now. When I was born, Mom was at university. She was taking an English course, as well as engineering courses.

I read in a magazine recently that Mr. Layton didn't care about his kids, only about his great career. That's what his son David said. So I guess the poem was hypocritical.

Sometimes I think my mother thinks more about her career than about me. Every summer for the past four years, I have gone to Grandma's house. I did this so Mom could live cheaply and study quietly. (She was taking her Master's degree.) I like going to Grandma's, but I don't like getting out of the way. I disappear not only so Mom can study, but also so she can spend time with Joe and Aunt Hanna.

Joe Dekkers is my mother's "manfriend", My mother is divorced from my father, whose name is Mark Janasiewicz. Mom left Dad before I was born. I have never met Dad. He lives in another country, and my parents can't afford to send me to visit him. Dad is a successful translator. But in his country, Poland, being successful doesn't mean you make much money.

Mrs. Henderson, you asked us to tell you about our greatest desire in life. Mine is to to be comfortable with myself. Happy with myself. I have no other goals. This bothers my mother. My second greatest desire is to meet my father. This also bothers my mother. In our family, we have a history of never seeing our fathers.

* * *

"What happened exactly 60 years ago, on September 10, 1939?" asked Mr. Dunlop yesterday in history class. Then he paused dramatically.

The pause got longer and longer.

Nobody could answer the question.

"Canada entered the Second World War," Mr. Dunlop said.

Nobody looked interested.

"I am shocked that none of you knew that," Mr. Dunlop went on. "Most of you have at least one grandfather or great uncle who fought in that war."

Then, for homework, he told us to interview a relative who has memories of the war.

I explained to Mr. Dunlop that the only older relative I have handy is my Aunt Hanna, who was just a little kid in Poland during the war. He said I should interview her anyway. I said I would do this. I did not tell him that I am not looking forward to the experience.

Mrs. Henderson, I hope you are not shocked by what I just wrote. I am only being honest. I have good reasons to be angry with Aunt Hanna. Furthermore, history seems like a boring subject to me. I prefer real life right now.

*   *   *

Clear blue Alberta sky and bright yellow summer sun. Turquoise water of the swimming pool. Grandma's backyard seems like a resort with a pool, deck chairs, tables and wide umbrellas for shade. There is even a bar for fancy drinks, such as "Pink Lady", and "Shirley Temple", and "Screwdriver".

Mom would be furious if she knew George invited me to drink alchohol sometimes, when Grandma wasn't around. Mom and Hanna don't drink at all, and neither does Joe. As for me, I don't like the taste

4

of liquor, so I don't touch the stuff, even when I'm invited to.

George definitely drinks too much, like Mom says. But I don't think Grandma takes too many pills, like Mom also says. Maybe she used to when Mom was my age, but she doesn't any more. Grandma says she's more confident than she used to be. I love Grandma. We see many things the same way.

Grandma only takes one drink before dinner. But George is really an alcoholic. He's not a wino on the street. He's rich and respectable, but he still has a drinking problem.

"He's been so depressed since Wayne Gretzky retired last winter," Grandma says.

"Maybe he's just bored with having nothing to do except golf," I say.

Grandma Whitehead (also known as "Maggy" or Magda) is in her fifties. George Whitehead (my step-grandfather) is in his sixties. George is a retired executive. All summer, he golfs around Edmonton. All winter, when he and Grandma go to Arizona or Hawaii, he golfs around those places.

They have "a nice life", Grandma says. "The Good Life", George says.

They bar-b-q pork, bar-b-q chicken, bar-b-q beef.

Mom says they eat too much meat.

I am diving, swimming, floating. I am lying on a beach towel and smelling the meat and listening to the music.

George listens to incredibly old singers like Pat Boone, Frank Sinatra and Dean Martin.

I listen to rap and heavy metal sometimes, and Puff

Daddy, Jay-Z, and Korn. But my favourite singer is Jann Arden. She has a soft voice and nice lyrics.

At Grandma's, I listen to the CDs that Grandma gives me the money to buy. My favourite CD right now is *Happy?* by Jann Arden. My favourite song on it is "Hangin' by a Thread". Jann is from Alberta. She makes up her own songs.

At Grandma's, I also watch TV shows like *Felicity, Friends, Dawson's Creek* and *South Park*. And John Candy movies.

At home, Mom and I don't have a CD player or TV, only an upright piano. That's why I catch up with normal stuff at Grandma's.

At Grandma's, I also go shopping for clothes. At home, Mom never lets me spend much money on stylish clothes. They have to be practical for school.

* * *

On the flight back to Toronto from Edmonton last week, I started humming Rita MacNeil's "Flyin' on Your Own". My mother likes this song, so when I think about her, I think about the song. Sitting beside me was an appealing guy. He looked a few years older than me. He was thin but muscular. He had sand-coloured, wavy hair and deep-blue eyes. The expression in his eyes was the loneliest I have ever seen. He was looking at the pictures of birds in a book called *John James Audubon: Writings and Drawings*. But he also kept glancing intensely at me.

"Sorry about the noise," I say to the guy.

"That's okay. I do solo vocals too," the guy says.

"You like music too? Wow! That's great!" I gush.

"My father had his own band when he was my age, and I've always wished I could too."

"Actually, I do bird calls," he says. "My father gave me some tapes of bird songs, and I'm learning how to imitate different species."

"I saw your address on your hand luggage," I say. "I live in Mapleville too. We probably go to the same school."

"I don't think I've seen you before," he says.

"Mom and I moved from the west end of town last June," I explain. "Mom bought a house near East Collegiate, so I could walk to high school, and she could walk to work. She teaches at the college. I don't know anybody who goes to East. Do you always read such huge books?"

"No," says the guy. "This was a present from my father too. I like drawing birds and other wildlife, so Dad thought I'd like this new book. And actually I do. Audubon was a famous bird painter in the States."

The guy's name is Curtis Brown. He's three years older than me. We talked for the whole flight. Or rather, I talked, and he listened. When we separated at the airport, he said he'd call me, but so far he hasn't. It's only been a week since we met, but already I am worried that maybe he won't call. I have never had a boyfriend before, and I think it's time I did. More importantly, I really like Curtis. He is unique.

Curtis

Woo-oo! Mysterious and lovely She Wolf sighted. Small. Feminine. Black, watchful eyes. Black, glossy hair.

7

What would she think if I told her about Dad? Would she tell other kids at school? Getting funny looks because I'm a bird watcher is bad enough. Forget the girl! Forget school! Just think about drawing.

Bye, Girl. Hi, Owl.

Hoo! Hoo!

Blink. Blink.

Eyes like orbs from outer space open into darkness. Golden and luminous.

Well hello there, my stuffed friend. How shall I draw thee? Let me count the ways. Let me count the feathers. Hundreds of bee-yoo-ti-ful feathers. One thin line, then another, then another. And then I'm gone. Into the golden eyes. Into the artwork.

I was looking at the drawing I did of a female downy woodpecker last summer, before I went to Dad's. I ran up to the bird just after it hit the picture window of our house. I watched the life fade from its eyes. I felt the body grow cold.

That was my best drawing yet. Naturally, Steve thought I was a wimp for spending hours doing it.

As I buried the bird, I got the strange idea that it had brought me a message.

What message?

Eva

I felt like the man who woke up one morning and found that he had become an insect. The man was in Franz Kafka's famous story, *The Metamorphosis*.

I found Hanna lying almost paralyzed in that little rented room in Montreal. I took her to the nearest hospital. The doctor said she had breast cancer that had spread to her spine. He showed me how her breast was becoming like a bleeding heart emerging from her chest. I began to scream silently. I was a huge, Kafka-esque insect, upside down, screaming silently.

After I boarded the bus to return home, I turned to the window, closed my eyes and silently screamed and screamed. The bus ride was about seven hours. For the first few hours, I was oblivious to my surroundings. I had no idea who was sitting beside me. Someone was beside me, however, because there was a persistant nudging. Nudge, nudge, nudge.

I continued to scream silently in the silence. I felt as though I were at the end of the Earth, in some far-off place too strange even for strangers. The nudging persisted. Eventually, I uncurled and straightened up. I was still at the end of the Earth. I was a huge insect, upside down at the end of the Earth, screaming silently.

A big old black woman was sitting beside me. It was she who had been nudging. That's who dwells at the end of the Earth, I found—an old woman in a bright, flowery dress and a pink Sunday hat.

She began talking, this woman. I could barely understand her, because her Jamaican accent was so thick. I can't remember what she said. Maybe she said: "Tell me what is wrong, child."

I said something. I don't know what. I can't remember. Maybe I said: "My sister is dying and she didn't tell me." Maybe I said: "My sister is like a mother to me."

We talked and talked for the rest of the trip. I don't remember what I said. She said she was working as a cook, and now she was going to her niece's wedding in Toronto. I don't know what else she said. Maybe she told me some of her own problems. How else could she have been so comforting? I only know that the talk seemed to carry me along. It was that old woman who carried me home, not the bus.

I returned home to Mapleville, only to go back again to Montreal as soon as possible. This time I took Joe's truck, so I could fetch Hanna and her few possessions, mostly papers.

In the months since then, I have tried to understand what happened to Hanna. Sometimes I weep, sometimes I am angry, and sometimes I want to run away. I open Hanna's boxes randomly and read the papers I find. Scribbled notes mostly. And various documents.

Hanna can't or won't talk about her experiences.

I didn't talk to the old woman again. I never saw her again after we said goodbye at the bus station. Rather, I talked to the nurses and my partner, Joe. I couldn't talk to Naomi. She was visiting her grandmother in Edmonton all summer. I didn't want to say anything on the telephone or in a letter. I didn't want to burden her. Naomi is too young.

Thank God for Joe! He is so solid, so kind, so patient, so strong. Never intrusive. Amazingly intuitive. I long to lie in his arms again.

What a balancing act Joe has to do! His ex-wife, who has custody of his sons, lives a few blocks away from him in one direction. His ex-wife supposedly loathes him, but nevertheless continues to expect his help in raising their sons. I live a block away from Joe in the opposite direction. I depend on him for emotional support.

Joe tells me not to be so obsessed with Hanna. How can I not be obsessed with Hanna? She is completely helpless now. Can't walk alone. Can't go to the toilet alone. She is in constant pain. She awakens in the night with pain. She is pale, gaunt and frail. Starved. The nurse says that Hanna has been suffering from malnutrition for a long time.

Joe

Eva's daughter is back, but meanwhile Eva is overwhelmed with caring for her sister. She should get more help. Naomi probably won't help much.

I'm back to the bachelor's lonely life. To the thwarted photographer's frustrated life.

The noctilucent cloud pictures I got with the old Pentax outside Winnipeg are pretty good. Eva thinks I might get a decent mercury barometer and weather vane from an antique dealer. I phoned the local dealers this afternoon, but had no luck.

I'll have to phone the Toronto dealers. But when will I get time to go to Toronto?

Jerry and Jeff start school this week too, of course, so now I will see them only on weekends. Maybe it's a good thing that I have to go back to teaching. I'll be too busy to mind the quiet around here.

Glad I gave up the extra union work. Class preparation, plus marking, plus all the departmental meetings are enough.

Have started T'ai Chi. John Van der Velden says it's great for improving flexibility and concentration.

11

Weekend street hockey with Jerry and Jeff won't be enough exercise.

John Van der V. has incredible photographic equipment. All new. Of course, he does not have kids!

Eva, you are a goddess in the moonlight. When shall we two meet again? I await your weather reports.

Week Two

Naomi

Saturday, September 18, 1999

I return from my perfect holidays. I discover that I have to sleep in this tiny, windowless room. The room is located behind the furnace, in a corner of our ugly, unfinished basement. The room was built this summer by Joe. My real bedroom is upstairs. It is near our bathroom and front door. That is why Hanna is lying in a hospital bed in my room.

Joe and Mom don't say anything about this change while we are driving along the highway from the Toronto airport. They only say there will be a "bit of a surprise". I don't ask if this will be a nice surprise, because I sense something is wrong. Mom is sad and quiet. Anyway, I don't usually talk much when Joe is around.

I answer Mom's questions about my holiday with single words like "Great!" and Fine!" Then I settle into polite silence until we get home, and until my mother and I are alone.

My mother is usually a strong woman who does

not depend on Joe, a sociology and psychology teacher at the college. Mom doesn't look like me at all. She is tall and chubby, and she dresses conservatively and practically. She wears suits and plain blouses that mix and match to make the perfect engineer-teacher's wardrobe. She is proud of her status as teaching staff in the Engineering Technology Department at the college. This high status is compatible with her basic self-image. Thus, she avoids frivolities like pink nail polish, frills like ruffles, and clutter like costume jewellery. These are the same frivolities, frills and clutter that Grandma and I consider absolutely necessary.

Anyway, I find out what the surprise is when, unsuspectingly, I walk in the front door, turn right in the front hall, enter my room, and see...

White, thin face. Long, greying, brown hair. Loose hair, foaming all over the pillow. Metal bars on sides of high hospital bed. Whole table by window filled with medical equipment like bed pan, surgical gauze, white tape, scissors, ointments, disinfectants. The only non-medical thing on the table is a green, potted, jade plant that used to be in the living room. It stretches toward the window for more light.

"Hanna?" I ask stupidly.

"Hello," she says. And love pours out at me from her greyish-blue eyes. I don't remember her eyes being so grey before. Can eyes get grey when you are sick?

"Hello," I say. I don't go and kiss her like I used to when I was a little kid. I just sort of smile wanly, wave and glide back into the front hall. Then I stare at Mom, who stares at me. Then Joe finishes bringing in

14

all my suitcases. (Grandma bought me two more suitcases to hold my new clothes.) Joe nods at me, kisses Mom on the cheek and leaves.

Mom puts her finger to her lips to tell me not to say anything. She shuts the front door quietly behind Joe. She says with this falsely cheerful voice: "Come and see the garden, darling. I have something to show you." We go out to the back of our little back yard, where there are no vegetables or flowers, only weeds. But at least Hanna can't hear us, so we can talk freely.

Mom and I have always been pretty good friends, but I feel that Mom betrayed me by not telling me what happened during the summer while I was away.

As payment for giving up my room and helping with Hanna, this is what I negotiated:

-I get to keep and wear all the clothes, plus the "frivolities, frills and clutter" that Grandma bought for me in Edmonton.

-I get to work part time during the school year, if I can find a job. And I can spend the money on anything I want, including a trip to somewhere warm at Christmas, if I can find somebody "responsible" to go with.

* * *

Mrs. Henderson, I just read what I wrote. I realize that I sound hard hearted. But I am not. Although Hanna is like a mother for my mother, I don't know her all that well. We haven't visited much for the past four years, since Mom and I moved to Mapleville. Even when I was a little kid, although Mom and I spent our holidays with Hanna, she was always remote. She was more like a teacher than an aunt. (No offense.)

One time when I went with Mom to visit Hanna in Montreal, Hanna had to make sure that we saw where the Oka Crisis was happening. She insisted that we go to where the Native warriors were camping, and where the army was patrolling with rifles and tanks. Hanna was very happy that Mom had rented a car to go to Montreal. She wasn't happy because we could drive to the St. Lawrence River to swim, or drive to the Laurentian Mountains to hike, but that we could drive to see Indians and soldiers staring at each other. This serious, scary stuff was more interesting for Hanna than the fun stuff that we also did.

Mom said Hanna's serious attitude toward life was a result of being born during a war and living under communism. I love Hanna. She has always been kind to me. Nevertheless, I feel closer to my mother's birth-mother, my grandmother in Edmonton. Grandma Whitehead is more normal because she was born right here in Canada, like me.

*   *   *

Last Tuesday evening when I got my tape recorder ready and went to interview Hanna about her memories of World War II, she just gave me her loving look and changed the subject.

"I remember a fairy tale from old Vienna about a basilisk at the bottom of a well," she said to me in French. "Have you heard this story?"

Hanna speaks French better than English. She talks

in that language and expects me to understand. Actually, I do understand, because I went to a French immersion school.

"No," I reply, feeling angry. "Look, Hanna, I need your memories of World War II for a school assignment for tomorrow. I don't have too much time…"

"Now this basilisk was croaking down at the bottom of the well," Hanna goes on, looking at the ceiling. "The croaking was a terrible sound. It sounded like a cross between a rooster, a frog and a serpent. And there was a terrible smell. Like rotten eggs. The townspeople thought of this strange animal as a monster. And indeed they were right. He was a horrible monster whose glance meant instant death…"

"Um, excuse me, please," I say politely, and I get up from my chair by Hanna's bed and switch off the tape recorder. "I've just remembered that I'm supposed to do something for Mom. I'll be back in a minute."

I go to see my mother in her bedroom, where she is making up an assignment for her students. Mom has a desk, computer, chair and filing cabinet in her bedroom, as well as a bed, bedside table and dresser. The room is small and crowded.

"Hanna isn't cooperating at all," I explain. "She's just telling me some fairy story, as though I'm still a little kid. I guess she just doesn't understand how urgent this is."

Mom sighs, takes off her glasses and rubs her eyes.

"Hanna senses your resentment of her, I'm sure," says Mom. "And your lack of understanding of her situation."

"How can I understand if nobody tells me anything?" I ask.

I am thinking that Mom looks tired.

Mom looks into my eyes. Then she nods.

"Last night I found this notebook of mine from twenty years ago," says Mom, getting up from her desk and going over to a heap of papers on her bedside table.

Mom hands me an ordinary school exercise book. There is writing on the first twenty pages or so. There is a yellowed article about Poland that Mom published in the *Edmonton Journal* a long time ago. Then there are blank pages.

"It's notes I made when I was visiting Poland in 1979. Turn to my visit to the Auschwitz Museum. You can copy what I said about that for your history assignment. I'm sure your teacher will be satisfied."

I spent an hour typing Mom's handwritten notes about Auschwitz. Even though I already knew about concentration camps from a film we had to watch in Grade Nine, I found Mom's comments heartrending. I handed the notes to Mr. Dunlop the next day.

* * *

I found out yesterday that Hanna does not have AIDS. So I don't have it.

* * *

Curtis has not phoned me yet. I am worried about him. Maybe he is having trouble in his life right now, like I am. He admitted that he had failed Grade Twelve last year, but he didn't say why. I should have talked less and listened more.

Curtis

No art class this year. I've taken all I can. Mr. Bell, the new physics teacher, is okay. In English we have to study a novel, plus stories, plus a play, plus poetry, plus writing skills. Nothing new there, or in the other courses. Should have passed Grade Twelve the first time.

The woodpecker tapped on my soul. Its message was, "To thine own self be true!" That's what Dad said on the phone last night. "If Audubon can spend seventeen years finding himself, you can fail Grade Twelve once, while you search for your vocation."

Dad says if I really want to be a wildlife artist, I should develop a portfolio in my spare time. But I still have to work at school. Or I won't get into art college.

"Bike out to the countryside and sketch on weekends," he says, "then concentrate on boring high-school subjects during the week."

I saw She Wolf in school, but she did not see me, because I ducked. She wears expensive clothes. Her grandparents are rich.

"You're a lone wolf," Mom always says. "It's not normal for a young man to spend so much time alone."

She never says what she is really thinking—that I'll turn out like Dad. She leaves that for the idiot drunkard, Steve.

Why did I come back from Dad's? Oh, yeah. He's got to build a new business and a new relationship now. He needs more time and space.

One day, Steve old man, you'll go too far. You hear that?

Lone Wolf has spoken.

Eva

I have been looking at the photograph album that Hanna once called "as precious as life itself". It is small. It fits in my hands. The photographs begin in the late 1930s.

A lovely, smiling, dark-haired woman in her twenties is leaning against a railing. This is Hanna's mother. A handsome, proud, sandy-haired man in his twenties is standing in front of a Christmas tree. This is Hanna's father. And mine.

There is a white, stucco house not so very different from houses I have seen here in Canada. It is not a mansion, but there is a sense of spaciousness—some lawn, a few trees.

There is another shot of rolling Polish countryside—I don't know where exactly in Poland. The fields and forest look like those here in southern Ontario.

In the first photograph of Hanna, she is a chubby, sturdy baby being lifted into the air by our paternal grandmother. Our grandmother looks proud but worried. In the second photo, our paternal grandfather is holding her. Hanna is reaching out for her mother. Our grandfather looks distracted.

There are no pictures of our father holding her because he was not there. Hanna was born in the autumn of 1939, after Poland had been invaded by Nazi Germany, after the Second World War had begun. Our father was away from home; he was fighting the enemy abroad. Neither of us ever saw our father, although we exchanged a few letters and spoke a few times on the telephone.

There is a photograph of our father in a pilot's uniform. You can hardly see his face for the goggles and tight helmet. At that time, he was in the Polish division of Britain's Royal Air Force. This is the last photograph of him in the album.

Except for photographs of Hanna being christened, and of an uncle posing in a soldier's uniform, there are no other pictures of the period of the war. There are no other pictures of our paternal grandparents. For some reason, there are no pictures of Hanna's maternal grandparents.

In a photo taken just after the war, Hanna is maybe six years old. She is walking hand-in-hand on a city street with her mother. Both are dressed nicely, rather formally.

Other pictures taken in the next few years are more casual. Hanna (seven?) and her mother are at the seashore with friends, having fun in the water. Hanna (eight?) is standing in a garden. Hanna (ten?) and a family friend are posing in the mountains in folk costumes.

There are no pictures of the terrible difficulties after the war. Only pictures of good things: flowers in a vase on a table, unidentified adults enjoying a picnic in the forest, unidentified family friends visiting for a few hours.

Then suddenly Hanna is a student. How old is she? Sixteen? Eighteen? She's at a table near a window. There are books and papers on the table, and she is writing or doing calculations. There is another picture of her a few years later. She is sitting in a field beside a saddle, looking pensive. Didn't she want to ride the horse?

Finally, she is a young woman. She is the same age as her mother was at the beginning of the album. She is not smiling, however. She is not looking at the camera. Her face is turned inward as she walks along. She is thinking.

Joe

Naomi is giving Eva a hard time about Hanna being in her bedroom. Why does Eva feel guilty about having made this arrangement? Eva is unsure of herself emotionally.

Strange how my ex-wife, Jill, exhibits so many of the superficial trappings of femininity: the makeup, the false fingernails, etc. Yet underneath Jill is cynical and tough.

I love Eva's freshness and fragility.

Hanna is just a few years older than me, yet she is dying.

My classes are going well. After twenty years of teaching, however, I am longing for a change. So many colleagues who started in the late 1960s, when the colleges first opened up, are taking early retirement now. They're my age.

I wonder if I can hold out for another ten years.

Eva is enthusiastic about teaching because she has been working in an engineering firm. When I started teaching, I had been counselling young offenders. Initially, teaching was a change: a new challenge.

Eva is almost twenty years younger than me! Does

it matter? No, we are truly in love.

Jill wants more money for the boys. They are involved in hockey, as well as baseball. Jill says I have no idea of the price of things today. I had to make do with second-hand stuff when I was a kid, so why can't the boys?

I wish the boys were interested in photography, so I could do some shoots on weekends. I missed a gorgeous sun pillar the other day because I didn't have my camera with me.

John Van der V. says some press in Toronto wants to publish a book of his astronomical photos. I'd love to do a book on weather.

All I need is a tornado!

Week Three

Naomi

Saturday, September 25, 1999

Mr. Dunlop was impressed with my mother's notes about the Auschwitz Museum. He read them to the whole class yesterday. Then he tried to start a discussion about the persecution of the Jews during World War II. Unfortunately, what happened next was totally embarrassing.

"During the Second World War, Jews were like people with AIDS today," says Mr. Dunlop. "Pariahs. Outcasts. Yet they were no different from you or me."

"I thought people with AIDS were homosexuals or drug addicts," says Bob Carter. "I don't know about you, sir, but I'm no fairy or dope fiend."

"No, you're just a ree-tard jock and beer-swilling jackass," mutters David Sutton.

The whole class hears David's remark and laughs. Even Mr. Dunlop smiles. Only Bob Carter scowls.

"Actually, you've got a point, Carter," says Mr. Dunlop. "One must be careful about making generalizations about groups of people. One must..."

"I wonder if Naomi is Jewish," says Melony Price. "Her first name is Jewish, and her last name is foreign."

"Thank heavens Mapleville is finally becoming a little more cosmopolitan," says Mr. Dunlop, as I feel my face turn hot and probably purple. "We need all the West Indians, Italians, Vietnamese and Greeks we can get to make this WASP enclave more interesting."

"Melony is just jealous because Mr. Dunlop picked Naomi's assignment to read out loud," says Sarah Smith.

Sarah sits behind me. She has waist-length blonde hair. She takes modelling lessons. She has gorgeous clothes. Plus she sings with a band!

"I'm not jealous," says Melony. "I was just stating facts. Naomi looks different, and her name is different."

"No more personal remarks, Melony," snaps Mr. Dunlop. "Such remarks lead to the same intolerance that got out of hand in Nazi Germany. Many people look 'different.' I do. You do. What is normal? Naomi is certainly 'normal'."

"Actually, I am one quarter Jewish," I burst out. "Supposedly, I look like my Jewish grandmother, my father's mother. My last name is Polish. My mother's grandparents came from Poland to Canada shortly after World War II. They were Christians, not Jews. I look like the women on that side of the family too. They also have dark hair and eyes."

"Thanks for taking Melony's remarks so well, Naomi," says Mr. Dunlop. "I'll bet your Jewish grandmother had a lot of stories about World War II. Authentic testimony..."

"I never met my Jewish grandmother," I say. "She

died before I was born. One of my grandfathers was a war hero. He was a pilot in the Polish wing of the British Air Force. One of my great-grandfathers was a partisan. That's an unofficial soldier in the Polish underground. My father's father was a journalist. I don't know whether he was a war correspondent or not. All these people died before I was born."

"I see I've got myself a first-class history student this year," says Mr. Dunlop, beaming.

"Not really," I say, feeling my face getting even hotter and purpler.

* * *

"I thought Melony was totally ignorant to pick on you like that," says Sarah after class as we're walking home.

History is our last class on Friday. We have walked partway home together each Friday since the beginning of the school year. Previous Fridays we talked politely about general topics. This Friday, we suddenly talked on a personal level, as though we were friends.

"Melony is as dumb as Bob," I say. "I hear they're going out together. They deserve each other. Actually, I was more embarrassed by Mr. Dunlop. Now he'll expect me to write brilliant essays or something, and I really don't care about school that much. I've got a job now, and I'm into fashion. I want to open a clothing boutique like my grandmother did after her kids grew up."

"You don't have to go to university for fashion," says Sarah. "But I think you still have to go to a community college."

"I don't want to go to university," I say. "Or college.

I'm not an intellectual like my parents and Aunt Hanna. Anyway, there are hardly any jobs for university graduates. It took my mother fifteen years after university to find a full-time job so she could raise me and buy a house. By the time Mom found the perfect job, I was already raised."

"Didn't you say that your father is a journalist?" asks Sarah.

"That's my grandfather. My father is a translator over in Poland," I say. "He used to translate for this guy called Lech Walesa. Walesa was a revolutionary leader who won the Nobel Prize for peace about twenty years ago. My parents are divorced."

"That sounds exciting," says Sarah, pausing at my ugly little red-brick bungalow. "I mean, about the Nobel Prize."

"It's not," I say. "Because I've never seen my father. He has another family. A wife and son. There's no contact at all. Not even letters. Mom hears news about him from an old aunt who still lives in Poland. This aunt has an apartment across the hall from my father's apartment. She is so old that she actually knew my father's parents and grandparents!"

"You could visit your father, couldn't you?" asks Sarah. "Poland isn't communist any more."

"Of course I could," I say, "if I had the money. And if he invited me. But so far he hasn't invited me. Mom thinks my father's present wife is jealous of me and won't let him see me."

"Is your Aunt Hanna really old?" says Sarah, flicking her long, perfect hair.

"Pretty old," I say. "Fifty-nine. She's a total invalid."

"That's awful," repeats Sarah. "My family is so boring compared to yours. My father calls us a FOOF: 'Fine Old Ontario Family. Pop, Mom, boy, girl. Healthy. Wealthy. Wise.' That's why I've got to get out of here. One more year, and Paris here I come. Or New York."

"I can see your name in lights now," I say. "TONIGHT: SARAH SMITH!"

"No, no! Too WASP! I'm changing my name to something Arab, or French, or..."

"How about Naomi Goralski?" I ask, smiling fakely.

"Hey! That's it! Jewish and Polish! How glamorous can you get?" Sarah says.

Sarah and I make a few more dumb name jokes, then she continues down the sidewalk to her gorgeous, gleaming, white, two-storey, Cape Cod house a few blocks away.

Sarah lives near where Curtis lives. One day I checked out their addresses in the phone book, and then I walked past Sarah's house. I was too embarrassed to walk past Curtis' house, so I don't know what it looks like. Curtis has not phoned me yet, so I suppose I was mistaken about the intensity of his glances at me. I am really disappointed that he has not called.

As I trudged up our cracked, weed-filled driveway to my run-down house, I was thinking that Sarah would have laughed hysterically if I had told her about my heartfelt desire to sing with her band and have a boyfriend.

* * *

"Hi!" I say to Hanna, leaning into my old room.

"Hello!" says Hanna. With a single word, she reveals that she is a foreigner. She pronounces *hello* like HALLO.

Her expression is gentle and sweet. This makes me feel guilty, but I still don't want to visit with her right now, so I rush off to the kitchen for a snack.

As I'm eating vanilla yoghurt mixed with sliced banana and granola, I pull my marked history assignment out of my backpack and read Mr. Dunlop's comments: "A+. This is outstanding. Maybe you would like to collect more of your family's memories of World War II for a longer, special project."

A+? Hey! I am not a bad student. I always pass. But this is my first A+! Trust my mother, the ace student, to get an A+. I get mostly Bs. My mother says I don't "apply myself". I could use an A+ in history. But unfortunately, there's nobody in my family to interview.

* * *

I started working last week. My job is cleaning at the Mapleville Recreation Complex, about six blocks from where we live. The job is hard. Huge mops. Heavy buckets of water. Dozens of toilets and sinks to scrub. Kilometres of walls and floors to wash. Minimum wage. Naturally. Weekends and holidays. Naturally. But I'm lucky to have any job.

If it weren't for Mary, I would have quit after the first hour. Mary is a medical doctor from Poland who is working as a cleaner because she's not licenced to practice medicine in Canada. Mary is older than Hanna: sixty-six. She is well dressed, sophisticated and humorous. She came to Canada eight years ago.

Mary has been cleaning full time at the Rec Plex for four years. She is my supervisor, but she helps me a lot. She doesn't just boss me.

Mary talks almost constantly as we are working together. She tries to teach me stuff by telling me funny little stories. At times, her stories are almost impossible to understand, because her English is so bad. I have to listen closely and get her to repeat words, so I can figure out what she is trying to say. She asks me to correct her English. But if I corrected every mistake, she'd never finish one single story in a whole eight-hour shift.

Mary says she's writing her life story for her grandchildren. I hope her Polish is better than her English!

* * *

I was leafing through a book about Poland that Hanna gave Mom a long time ago. The book was in English. It was called, *Poland: A Tourist Guide*. I was wondering whether it might have some quotes I could use for my history class. This is what the book said about the Jews during World War II: "The Jewish population of Warsaw was walled up in the Ghetto in 1940. Condemned to extermination, the Jews entered the unequal struggle. The Ghetto Uprising broke out on April 19, 1943 and continued till May 16, 1943. Unspeakable terror ruled the city."

Mom says that about six million Polish people died during World War II. This was about one quarter of the total population of Poland. About three million of these people were Jewish, and about three million were not Jewish. The ones who were not Jewish were mostly Christians. Mom says that many people today, possibly including Mr. Dunlop, do not know about the "horrendous death toll" of Polish Christians.

Mom says she has a book called *The Forgotten Holocaust* that I should read some day. It is about the three million, non-Jewish Poles who were murdered during World War II. The author of the book is Richard Lukas. Mom gave me a copy of this quote from the book: "On August 22, 1939, a few days before the official start of World War II, Hitler authorized his commanders to kill 'without pity or mercy, all men, women, and children of Polish descent or language'."

Mom thinks Mr. Dunlop might be interested in seeing this quote.

Curtis

Mom and Steve have broken up because of me. He finally did it. Got even more drunk than usual and called me a "faggot" for not liking sports. I had politely asked him to please turn down the football game that he was watching on TV in the living room. I had explained that the noise was bothering me in my room.

"So whaddaya do for hours in your room?" he asks.

"He's painting animals for his art portfolio," says Mom. "He biked up to the wildlife park to do sketches of the animals, and now he's making paintings. Like

Robert Bateman. He saw a TV program about Bateman, and he got really inspired. He's always loved animals and art."

"All those artist types are faggots," says Steve. "Including Curtis-pooh here."

"Why don't you just get out of here," I yell. "What makes you think you have the right to hang around here anyway? Do you think you *own* my mother?"

"Ah, shaddup!" the moron says, and turns the volume up on the TV. "Why'd ya hafta come back here anyway? I thought you and your fairy father were having a great time. Your Mom and I sure were."

At that point, I rush him and get him by his idiotic bull neck. Steve, who has been working for a moving company and lifting incredible weights, shoves me off him, lunges after me, kicks me in the shin and punches me in the gut before I can get away from him.

Mom screams, runs to the kitchen, and dials 911. Before the police get here, Steve staggers out the front door, gets in his car and roars away.

I am still in pain when the police arrive, but nothing is broken, so Mom refuses to press charges. She also begs me not to. She says Steve's upset because he lost his job.

Now Mom is depressed about Steve leaving. My fault, I suppose. Too bad.

Mary

Seeds

If you look at seeds up close, they are as big as boulders. But they are so light, you can blow them away with one breath. Daddy carefully saves our seeds from the year before. Seeds are like tiny sleeping giants.

All through the long winter, when the snow is as high as our house, the seeds wait in the darkness and warmth of our barn. Sometimes I go look at them. I take a few in my hand. I blow on them as gently as a spring breeze.

Mostly, though, I don't think about anything except having fun. Johnny is fun. He is my brother. He is one year older than me. Elizabeth, my sister, is two years older than me. She's not fun, she's a goody-goody. She says I'm not ladylike. Agnes, my other sister, is twelve years older than me. She's all grown up. She has gentleman friends who come to call. Agnes says I'm a little beast.

The snow's so high, we can climb up on the roof. Somebody left a ladder.

"We're birds. Let's fly," says Johnny.

We jump off the roof into the snow. We are buried in the snow! We crawl out.

Mommy bangs on the window and shakes her finger at us. Then she rushes outside, wiping her hands on her apron.

"Don't do that!" she cries. "You might get hurt or lost in the snow. And then you'd be frozen, and we wouldn't find you."

"Mommy," says Johnny, running up to the door. "We're hungry. Can we have those cold pancakes?"

"Here," says Mommy, handing him the leftover potato pancakes from lunch. "And stay out of trouble."

"Come on, Mary," Johnny says to me, after Mommy has closed the door. "We're arctic explorers. Let's go for a ride."

Carrying our pancakes, we run to the barn. We tie our big dog Bear to our little sleigh. Then we get into the sleigh. Then we throw pieces of pancake ahead of Bear in the snow. Bear runs ahead to find his pancake treats. He pulls us along in the sleigh.

Bear pulls us across the fields to the edge of the forest. Then he stops because we have no more pancake pieces to throw.

Bear refuses to pull the sleigh any more. He sits down. When Johnny takes the rope off his neck, Bear runs away.

"What will we do?" I ask. "It's a long way home, and I'm getting cold."

"We'll pull the sleigh ourselves," says Johnny. "You'll soon warm up."

And we did, and I do. But it takes us a long time to get home through the deep snow. We are late for dinner, and I am cold again.

Mommy rubs my hands and feet with snow. She gives me boiling hot raspberry tea to drink. Then she shakes her finger at us again and says: "Don't do that! See how cold Mary is! She's almost frozen! Now go to your rooms, both of you. And stay there all evening! And no visiting!"

Another day, when the snow is almost gone, but it is still cold, Johnny and I lean against the sunny side of the house, where it's warmer. But we're still cold, so we gather little sticks and dead grass, and we light a fire with some matches that we took when Mommy wasn't looking.

The fire is going nicely. Our hands are getting toasty warm. Then along comes Mommy with a basket of laundry for the clothesline.

She drops the laundry, runs for a bucket of water, and throws the water on our fire. Then, surprise! Mommy does not shake her finger at us and say, "Don't do that!"

Instead, she says: "I am finished with you two. I've had enough of your mischief. Go out into the world. Then you'd see how lucky you are. You two have been very, very bad." Then Mommy spanks Johnny hard on the bum with her hand.

Then she spanks my bum just as hard.

And then she huffs off into the house and slams the door. She's left the laundry sitting in its basket in the yard, and she is so angry that she doesn't care.

"Let's run away," says Johnny, when we've finished bawling.

We run away to the barn.

We have a secret hiding place in the barn. It's made of straw and an old horse blanket. Nobody knows where we are. We stay there for hours and hours, all afternoon. We fall asleep. Then we wake up and hear Mommy calling us for dinner. But we don't come out.

Then Daddy finds us somehow.

"We're never going home again," says Johnny.

"Mommy spanked us. She told us to go out into the world," I say.

Daddy sits in the straw between Johnny and me, and puts his arms around both of us. "Now children," Daddy says, "your mother is not a young woman. Nor am I a young man. You are our second family, you know."

"What does that mean, Daddy?" I ask, snuggling into his coat.

"That means there was a war long ago, before you were born," explains Daddy, holding me close. "And our first two children, a boy and a girl, died because there was not enough food and no medicine. Only Agnes survived. She was the youngest, like you, Tiny Mouse. After the war, I had to go away for ten years to the United States of America. I had to earn money, so your mother and I could start all over again."

"Did Mommy miss her son after he died?" asks Johnny.

"She grieved and grieved and almost died herself," says Daddy. "Not until you were born was she the least bit happy again."

"Did Mommy miss her daughter after she died?" I ask.

"She grieved and grieved and almost died herself," says Daddy. "Not until Elizabeth was born was she the least bit happy again."

"Was Mommy happy when I was born?" I ask. Then I hold my breath.

"You, Tiny Mouse, were a surprise," says Daddy, hugging me and kissing the top of my head. "You were our valentine, and you made Mommy and me as happy as happy can be."

"Goody!" I say, and we all go home to hug and kiss Mommy.

When I am hugging Mommy, I say, "I am your valentine!"

Mommy laughs and says,"No, you're the old hen's chicky chick chick!"

"KOOKEREE KOO!" I crow like a rooster. "The old hen laid an Easter egg!"

"That's right," says Daddy. "It will be Easter soon. And soon time to plant seeds."

"I'll help you!" I shout.

"What about helping me?" asks Mommy. "I have twelve courses to prepare for Easter dinner. Then there are the eggs to decorate."

"Goody!" I shout, dancing a little polka around the kitchen. "Sausages and eggs! I can't wait."

"Well, you must wait," says Mommy, putting on her apron. "No meat for anyone for four weeks before Easter. And no butter, only oil for cooking."

And soon my brother and I are tapping our Easter eggs together.

"If you break my egg, you have to give yours to me," says Johnny. "If I break your egg, I have to give mine to you."

And we eat our eggs with salt. And we also eat sausages and fish and many other delicious things.

And we go to church. And the the priest blesses us all.

Eva

Hanna left Poland in 1979. She never returned. She stayed with me for several years at my Grandma Goralski's house in Edmonton, until I was established in my engineering studies.

After martial law was declared in Poland in December 1981, she was able to get landed immigrant status in Canada quickly, and then she looked for work. She found temporary, full-time, contract work for three years in Montreal, developing the Polish collection of a special new library devoted to Slavic culture and history. I stayed in Edmonton to finish my degree and look after my grandmother.

After the Solidarity Uprising in August 1980, I saw Mark regularly on television broadcasts from Poland. He was translating for the leaders of the Solidarity movement. (He was very cynical when I knew him in Warsaw, but he finally decided that he believed in something!) I only met Mark once again—in Canada. He came to raise money here for Solidarity. He got in touch with me when he arrived in Edmonton. We went out for dinner and spent the night together.

Why? Because what Mark was doing was so romantic? Because Jake Wiens, the fellow I liked, had fallen in love with my friend Alice, not me? Unbelievably, I became pregnant just from that one intimacy. Believably, when I wrote Mark about Naomi, he wrote me that he had a wife and baby son in Warsaw. I wrote him that I wanted a child but no husband. He never wrote back. For a few years, I secretly longed for Mark. Then I fantasized about shooting him. Now my anger is gone. I love Joe.

Grandma Goralski died before Naomi was born. My mother helped look after the baby until I finished my degree, but we still didn't get along. Then I moved East to be near Hanna.

Joe

The boys are crazy about hockey. (Must come from Jill's side.) Took them to an exhibition game on Saturday afternoon. Spent most of Sunday afternoon messing around with tennis balls and hockey sticks on the asphalt of the school yard.

The boys said Jill finally has a steady boyfriend. She was at his house while the boys were with me. They said he's a jerk, but they won't explain. Just loyalty to me?

Eva was right. The boys liked the Sloppy Joes from her ground meat sauce equally as well as take-out burgers, and the "Joes" are cheaper and more nutritious. The boys approve of Eva. She's "cool." Of course, there hasn't been much opportunity for them to get to know her.

No time this week for the camera and dark room. Would love to go up to Algonquin Park and capture some fall colours and clear, sunny northern skies. Fat chance.

My classes are going well, but I am sick and tired of the discipline problems. These kids straight out of high school from comfortable homes are a bore—boozing, partying, skipping class, mouthing off. Two years minimum travelling and working experience between high school and college should be mandatory.

I'm making a list of photographic challenges to be met as soon as possible. These include all different types of clouds; all possible phenomena, such as sun pillars, sun dogs, halos around sun and moon and rainbows; lightning during a thunderstorm; etc.

The shots of lenticular clouds over the mountains near Calgary are not up to book standard.

Eva says maybe she can find an old hydrometer for me somewhere.

Week Four

Naomi

Saturday, October 2, 1999

Mom is preoccupied with Hanna. Hanna can't get out of bed at all, and she often won't eat anything. Of course, Mom is also busy with teaching at the college. Mom says that, with all the cutbacks these days, plus so many early retirements, there are double the usual number of students per class. Also she has two new courses: Robotics and Computer Interfacing.

Mom is gaining weight from eating too much while she cooks on Saturdays, and from not doing her yoga exercises at home. She knows she should go to a fitness centre like the Rec Plex and work out in a group, but she can't afford the membership fee. Furthermore, she doesn't have time. At least, she walks to and from work.

"Consumed with guilt." That's what Joe says is wrong with Mom. I really don't see why Mom should feel guilty about Hanna.

I heard Mom talking to a nurse about something I was not supposed to know about. They were over by the big freezer, which is on the opposite side of the basement from my room, and on the opposite side of the house from Hanna's room. It was so early in the morning that they thought I was still asleep. The nurses come to change Hanna's dressing about six in the morning. Then they take care of Mom by talking to her or listening.

"Hanna's mother committed suicide at the same age for similar reasons," says Mom. "She thought the world was too evil. Her loved ones had died or gone away."

Mom's voice is high and tight. She pauses, but the nurse does not say anything.

"After two young friends died...they died of AIDS...Hanna lost all interest in life. Even before that, she was becoming mentally ill. This happened over four or five years."

Another pause, but still the nurse does not say anything.

"Now she says she wants to die. She wants pills or something. She says it's cruel to continue this way. She doesn't want all this help. She wants euthanasia."

"I'll talk to the doctor about this," says the nurse. "Maybe I can get him to visit her."

"Could you?" asks Mom. "Oh, thank you."

"You need more rest, Eva," says the nurse. "Take a break now and then. Have the people from Hospice Mapleville been coming?"

41

"Yes," says Mom. "A volunteer came on Sunday, so Joe and I could get away for a few hours. But Hanna doesn't like strangers here. She'd rather be alone. She doesn't trust strangers. She thinks they're spies."

"She shouldn't be left alone," says the nurse. "She's completely helpless. She can't even reach for a glass of water."

"I know," says Mom.

My alarm goes off. Supposedly to wake me up, so I'll be on time for work. Mom and the nurse go upstairs. I'm really glad I'll be with Mary all day, because I can talk to her as much as I want. We're getting to be good friends.

I don't tell Mom that I overheard her, because it's better if she doesn't think I'm upset. She goes crazy if she thinks there's something wrong with me. She's overprotective, because I'm an only child, and because she didn't have normal mothering herself.

While she was growing up, Mom mainly had her strict grandmother: my Great-grandmother Goralski. Then, after she was already eighteen, Mom had Aunt Hanna. Mom lived with her mother, my Grandma Maggy in Edmonton, only for two years. One year was when she was a baby, and one year was when she was about my age. Mom was an illegitimate child. "When my mother was young," Mom says, "she wanted to marry George and get on with her life. She didn't want her mistake staring her in the face every day."

Actually, I was an illegitimate child too, but I don't usually tell people. Now you know secret information about me.

Mom believes in "thinking for oneself." Independence of mind is very important to her, Joe, and Hanna. Those three think for themselves all the time. But I believe that a person needs to stop thinking sometimes and relax. I relax by visiting Grandma Maggy.

Sometimes I worry that Mom is going to have a nervous breakdown from thinking too much. She is too tense. She tries to be a teacher at home as well as at the college. Mom represses too many of her emotions, so she can remain efficient at all times.

Mom works incredibly hard. "I am very lucky to finally have a good, full-time job," she says. "All my colleagues are men, and there's never been a woman instructor in this department before, except for the 'frill' courses like English. I have to do everything as well as a man would. But I still have to run a household and look okay."

These days, for example, Mom leaves the house at 7:30 a.m., and she is not back until 5:30 p.m. I'm supposed to make lunch for Hanna and me, and to prepare everybody's dinner. Making dinner usually means taking a frozen casserole out of the freezer and putting it in the oven. It also means making a salad, setting the table and preparing a tray for Hanna. Mom makes casseroles and stuff like spaghetti sauce on Saturdays.

Mom eats dinner with me at the kitchen table. Supposedly, this is so we can talk, but I find we don't really talk the way we used to, because we both try to hide our true feelings from each other. Then, while I do the dishes and my school work, she does college work in her room for a couple of hours. She doesn't get a chance to visit with Hanna until about 9:30 p.m. When she sits beside Hanna's bed, neither of them talk much. Both were always silent types. They're alike in many ways.

"Focussed, professional women," Joe once called them. He called *me* a "scatterbrained glamour girl." He was joking, but I didn't appreciate his sense of humour.

Mom leans her head against the rail of Hanna's hospital bed. She dozes, I think, but Hanna doesn't mind. Mom goes to bed at ten, but she wakes up at night and wanders around the house, or looks in Hanna's boxes, or writes in her journal, or does more school work.

* * *

Here is a typical dinner table conversation between my mother and me:

"So how was your day, dear," says Eva.

"Fine," says Naomi.

"Did you get a chance to practice music after school?" says Eva.

"No. I've given up on music," says Naomi. "I've got too much to do with work and school." (I haven't, but I'm not going to admit to her that I lay on my bed in my room for two hours, wondering about why Curtis didn't even say "Hi!" when I finally passed him in the hallway at school.)

"You know you don't really need this job at the Rec Plex," says Eva. "If your school work suffers, you'll have to quit. I see too many kids at the college missing their year because they're overextended."

"I thought you said a lot of your students party all the time," Naomi says. "I never party, because I don't have any friends. Except maybe this girl called Sarah at school. I told you my best friend Pam moved to Vancouver with her family last summer. She never writes. Also I don't care about my old gang at my old school. The girls just giggle and talk about boys they don't know. The boys just talk about getting drunk or doing weed."

"I know from personal experience that being an only child makes it difficult to interact with one's peers," says Eva, sounding like a text book. "I'm glad you've been spending summers with my mother. She is very different from me. But it's too bad that there are no other people your own age in Grandma's neighbourhood. And no cousins. If Gord has fathered children, I suppose we'll never hear about them. He's become a drifter. High school drop out. Can't hold down a job.... It's his drinking. Magda never could face George's alchoholism, or Gord's."

"Um, could you please pass the ketchup," Naomi says and changes the topic of conversation to her new job.

Naomi thinks her mother is jealous of her grandmother's love for Gord. Uncle Gord is actually quite funny, even if he is a "lazy good-for-nothing who lives off any woman who will have him." That's what his own father, George, says about him.

*   *   *

Mrs. Henderson, please tell me if the following is acceptable for the poem we have to write for English.

The Blind Man's Song

Where is the sadness in this misery?
Where is my pain?
I am walking in the rain.
I am walking with a blind man's cane.

It's so far to go.
It's so long to wait.
It's so hard to see.
It's getting so late.

In the other place over by the gate,
in the other place over by the river,
in the other place, in the other place,
there's got to be some space to play in
some way to stay away from
the things that confound you, confuse you,
refuse to let you be free;
to find that place inside
that never goes away.

That never goes away,
that waits
to see if you'll come back
before it's too late.

Before the gate is closed,
before the river runs no more, before there's

no place left to go.
Go back and find your inside space!
Stay away from
the things that confuse you, confound you,
and refuse to let you be free.
Find that place that
never goes away.

Where is the sadness in this misery?
Where is my pain?
I am walking in the rain.
I am walking with a blind man's cane.

Curtis

Steve pounds on our door today, while Mom and I are eating supper. I look out the living room window. Steve's face is puffy and red, so I know he has been drinking. I tell Mom not to let him in.

"Go away!" Mom yells through the door.

"Open the door!" Steve yells back, and then he starts swearing and kicking the door.

"Go away!" Mom yells again.

Steve keeps swearing and kicking. I am about to call the cops. Mom stops me.

"It's okay," she says. "He's going away."

"We should call the police anyway," I say. "We should get a restraining order."

"Steve won't hurt us," she says.

"You're naïve," I say. "You're not a good judge of character."

"Don't you dare talk to me like that!" she says.

"Just because I'm young doesn't mean I'm stupid," I say.

"Are you calling *me* stupid?" she yells. "You failed your school year!"

"I failed my school year because you and Dad fight all the time, and because I can't stand Steve," I say. "Dad is a lot more intelligent than Steve. I wish Dad had never left."

"It wasn't my fault your father left," she yells. "And at least Steve is *normal*."

"You were incredibly cruel and unfair to Dad," I say. "You made him feel totally depressed. Steve is an idiot. A low-life. A know-nothing."

Mom storms off to her room and slams her door.

Mary

Medicine

When my oldest brother and sister died, Mommy didn't know about medicine, because she was very young, not much older than Agnes is today. But now Mommy knows, because she's more than forty. Almost fifty!

This morning, I went with Mommy to gather plants in the forest to make medicine. The plants were ready for picking, and Agnes was too busy getting ready for her birthday party, and Elizabeth didn't want to get dirty, and Johnny was helping Daddy in the barn. I like running through the fields and the forest, looking for exactly the right leaf or flower. I'm good at this, and I don't care if I get dirty. Mommy says I can go with her all the time now, instead of Agnes or Elizabeth.

I don't care if Elizabeth says my socks are falling down, and my hair is messy. I don't even care if Agnes says I am a beast.

Elizabeth has beautiful, natural, golden curls. She is perfectly composed. She always looks in the mirror before she greets her guests, because that is what Agnes does. Agnes has beautiful, natural, golden curls too.

My hair is plain brown and straight. Elizabeth says I have "piggy piggy piggy pig tails."

Agnes isn't ready yet when her gentleman friend comes to the front door. He comes far too early for the party, yet he thinks he's smart because he's already at medical school. Agnes is going to go to medical school next fall. She's going to graduate from high school next week. So this is a party for her birthday and graduation. It's very important.

When Agnes's gentleman friend knocks on the front door, Agnes knows who it is because she peeks through the window. She says to me, "Go and tell him I'm not here yet."

I run to the front door and open it.

"Agnes says to tell you she's not here yet," I shout. Then I slam the door shut.

"B-e-a-s-s-s-t!" Agnes hisses at me, when I run back to tell her what I told him. Agnes has already heard what I told him, and she doesn't like it. I don't know why.

I don't care what Agnes says. I'm already learning about medicine with Mommy, so I'll be a doctor too.

And I'll be floating through the birch trees in the middle of the night, like Agnes. It looks magical down there. The lanterns are lighting up the white trees and the white dresses. It sounds magical down there too.

The music on the gramophone is romantic. Agnes's gentleman friend comes back at the right time. He brings her a present. The other ladies and gentlemen come too, and now they're all dancing. Dancing and dancing through the magical night.

I'll dance like that some day too. I love dancing, and I'm very good at gymnastics and other sports. That's what Daddy says. He says it's amazing how I can climb to the very top of the trees to pick apples. I'm like a squirrel, he says. And I'm as fast as a rabbit.

But you know what happens after that night of Agnes's party? The very next day, after they clear away the lanterns, the wind begins moaning in the birch trees. The white birch trees begin moaning like ghosts. Grandpa comes to visit us that day. The moaning goes on and on. It gets louder and louder. Grandpa shakes his head and says: "There will be war again soon. You mark my words."

Agnes does not go to medical school that fall, or ever. War comes on the first day of September. Nazi Germany invades Poland. And soon Agnes is sent away to Germany to work like a slave in a factory, building bombs and making bullets. I do not see Agnes again until she is an old woman. She lives in Canada then, and she comes to visit me in Poland. We laugh together about what I said to her gentleman friend, and what she said to me. But that is much later. A whole lifetime later.

Meanwhile, that spring and summer and fall long ago, I help Mommy gather leaves and flowers and bark. I help her make medicine. It's a good thing I do, because when the war begins, the enemy is wounding our friends, neighbours and relatives. And all the doctors and pharmacists have gone away with the Polish army, or else they have been killed.

My Daddy has also gone away with the Polish army, and my Grandpa has come to live with us.

I help people, like Mommy does. One night before the village doctor goes away, I am visiting a neighbour lady. She swallows eye medicine by mistake, because she thinks it is her heart medicine. She wants to ask the doctor what to do.

The lady says to me: "If I die on the way, and I am alone, no one will tell my family what happened to me. I'm big and fat, but you're thin and small. No one will notice you, Mary."

So I go with her.

Soldiers go by on patrol as we creep along. I hear the squeaking of their heavy boots as they march along in the snow. We press ourselves into a hole in the fence, and the soldiers pass without seeing us.

Finally, we reach the doctor's house. The lady knocks, but the doctor will not open his door.

It is very dangerous to open your door at night.

Through the closed door, the lady explains her problem, and the doctor says that the medicine the lady swallowed will not hurt her.

"Humph!" the lady says after we get back safely to her home. "I should have asked your mother! She lives closer, and *she* would have opened her door!"

I am Mommy's helper. She takes me with her when she delivers food and medicine to poor people. We have to go at night because the enemy will see us during the day.

"How will we find our way?" I ask Mommy.

"By the moon on the snow," says Mommy.

And now it's spring again and warm. Soon we'll start looking for plants and bark.

A man with a terrible leg wound comes to our house. The wound looks horrible. It is full of pus.

"It is infected," Mommy says to the man. "I have no medicine left, but I'll reopen the wound to drain. Then you go lie in the sun."

While the man is lying there, our dog Bear comes and licks the wound. The infection disappears, and the wound heals in a few days.

"Dogs have natural medicine in their mouth," Mommy says.

Eva

There is a second photograph album—mine. Of course, it is also precious. In my album, there is only one photograph of Hanna in Poland. She is wearing a red blouse that I gave her. The blouse has white suns coming out from black clouds.

There are some photos of Hanna and I together in Canada. We are standing side by side in a camera store, not saying "cheese." We are sitting side by side in chairs, looking at a lake. We are sitting side by side on a bench, enjoying a park.

I keep looking at these beloved pictures to search for clues as to when and why Hanna became ill. When did she lose hope? What was the objective reality that caused her to become physically and mentally ill?

Increasingly, we saw each other only during

vacations. In the past four years, I have gone to Montreal without Naomi. Hanna was unemployed for a long time, and for a long time she refused to take welfare, so she had no reserves. I gave Hanna as much money as I could, and I stocked her cupboard with non-perishable groceries.

Hanna and I had grown apart. We lived about six hundred kilometres from each other. We had separate friends, separate activities, separate goals.

This is natural after a child has grown up—even an "inner child," which is what I was with Hanna. Also, I guess I was rebelling a little. I resented Hanna's saying I was becoming too materialistic. I felt I was doing what I had to do, laying a base for my financial security, for Naomi's future. How can you raise a child on the wages from part-time or temporary work?

But Hanna and I remained vitally connected. We talked on the telephone often. I told her about my work problems, my babysitter problems, my child problems. Her few words—with me she was always a listener, not a talker—were always the right words. A stranger herself, she guided me through this strange land. Truly, she was like a mother to me. A wise woman.

There is a photograph that I can hardly bear to look at. It was taken after I started to work at the college, study for the Master's degree, and go out with Joe. In Hanna's eyes, there is terrible grief and exhaustion.

* * *

The mental illness grew slowly. There were little signs of it for several years.

She began to claim that people were following her. She also claimed that, when she was attending a community college in Montreal, someone poured chemicals on her from above. She claimed that, when she was getting off a bus, someone jabbed her with a needle. "Maybe the needle had AIDS in it," she said.

The person sitting beside me on the bus to Montreal was a spy, she claimed, even though she herself had not been on the bus. The police were out to get her, she claimed, so they would try to get me. The police got a young friend of hers at the college, she claimed, because the young friend tried to help her.

At the time, I thought her claims were nonsensical. I thought they were symptoms of illness.

"This is paranoia," I said to Hanna. "These suspicions are crazy. This is not Nazi Germany. This is not Stalinist Poland. This is modern Canada. You worry too much. You are not eating right. You are identifying with your mother. You should see a doctor."

She would not talk in her apartment. This was not new. This was a holdover from the past in Poland, when the apartment could be "bugged" with listening devices. When we went outside, and she did begin to talk, the words became crazier and crazier.

"There is a conspiracy," she would say. "Multinational companies, drug companies. Capitalism is as bad as Nazism. I went to the hospital, and I saw that they just leave people in the hallways to die. I met my young friend there, my first adopted son. I kidnapped him from the hospital."

"The hospitals are overcrowded," I would say. "That's all. You need help. You need a doctor. You need a decent job. I found you a job near where I work, but you wouldn't take it. Why?"

"I don't need help," she would say. "I must stay here. I must stay with my people."

"Maybe you should go back to Poland," I would say. "Maybe you would feel better there. Your difficulties in Canada are driving you mad. That horrible job sewing in the garment district—what happened? Did someone hurt you? Why won't you talk about it? Why didn't you tell me?"

"Nothing happened," she said.

"But after that you were never the same," I said.

"The job with the 'artistic pictures' was just as bad," she said.

"You didn't tell me about that either," I said. "You are always trying to protect me. You should have asked me what 'artistic pictures' means here. How could you know they were making pornographic calendars?"

"Nothing happened. I left as soon as I saw what they were doing."

"*Something* happened! *Something* is wrong with you! This has come from the past. This is not Canada today. You need help. Let me get help for you."

"The doctors are in it too. You can't trust them. I can't leave my people. I belong here. I belong among the poorest of the poor. Young people here have no hope for a decent future. I have seen the suicide statistics for young people."

"We are in a new society. Canada is very different from Poland. We can't judge what is happening here. We just need to concentrate on ourselves, on putting down roots."

"I am staying here in Montreal. In the poorest district. These are my people. The poorest French Canadians are my people. The young, the unemployed, the sick are my people. Maybe I can do something here."

Finally, I went to my own doctor in Mapleville to get advice about Hanna. My doctor is an English Canadian. He is one of these typical doctors who is finished with you in two minutes, because he's processing one hundred patients a day. I made an appointment for myself for a complete checkup, so I'd have a whole ten minutes. I spent my time describing Hanna's symptoms.

"It is very difficult for me to judge your sister's condition without examining her," my doctor commented. "Then too there are cultural differences. My initial impression is that she has some sort of Christ complex, but don't quote me on that. I mean, she thinks she has to behave like Christ. Anyway, here in Canada it is difficult to commit a person to a psychiatric hospital without his or her consent. The only way one can do this is by proving that the person is going to harm himself or someone else. And that 'harm' has to be serious...like suicide or murder. Has your sister attempted suicide? Don't forget that you need irrefutable proof, such as evidence from a police officer or social worker. Can you take a policeman with you next time you visit her?"

I couldn't take a policeman, of course, because Hanna was so paranoid about the Quebec police. And my French wasn't good enough that I could seek a social worker in Montreal.

* * *

Now I wonder whether Hanna had objective reasons to be paranoid about the police. Tonight I found the following note among the boxes:

Thursday, May 3 about eleven o'clock in the evening, in front of the door of Apartment ____ in building ____ on ____ Street (near the corner of ____ Street and ____ Avenue), I was witness to a scene of police brutality (five big policemen against one person outstretched on the floor, feet tied).

This bleeding person (there were spots of blood in the corridor), was rolled up to his hair in a blanket, was deposited like a package on the edge of the sidewalk before being placed in police car no. ____.

At least six people besides me were present in the corridor of the third floor during the event.

I should like to have contact with the person arrested, his lawyer and a woman who happened to be in front of Apartment ____ at the moment described above.

I believe that I perhaps know the arrested person and could give testimony in his favour.

Joe

Eva was crying on the phone this evening abo~
sister wanting to die. Eva seems so stror
suddenly breaks down. All I could do wa

57

Gave Jill one thousand dollars—the last of the money earned by driving trucks all summer. And the academic year has barely started! I suggested to Jill that I should have some say in where she spends the money I give her, but of course she told me to "F--- off."

I can't stand that woman's vulgarity. How did I get involved? Forty-year-old, bald guy with no self confidence due to failed first marriage meets scheming female. That's how.

Eva is so selfless. I suppose she gets that from her role model, Hanna. Eva spends the minimum on herself. Naomi is such a contrast.

I lusted after gorgeous alto cumulus clouds this morning while walking to work.

Week Five

Naomi

Monday, October 11, 1999

"Grey on grey!" That is what I said to myself when I first saw Mary. Grey hair, grey eyes, grey face. Her entire body beamed, "Unhappy! Unhappy! Unhappy!" She was like a lighthouse in the rain. But she was also stylish and graceful. Now I know that she makes her own clothes, and that she did gymnastics when she was young. She was even supposed to be in the Olympics when she was my age, but she got sick and couldn't. Even though she is poor, she is always well dressed and attractive.

Mary talked to me nonstop from the minute I started working with her. Even though I know some Polish words from listening to Mom and Hanna, I found Mary hard to understand at first. One day, for example, Mary talked on and on about some guy called "Pop-yeh-woosh-ko". He was a Polish priest who was murdered. Mary's English was so bad that I thought this was something that happened during

World War II. But later, when I asked Mom if she knew about "Pop-yeh-woosh-ko", Mom explained that he was murdered only about fifteen years ago, in 1984, during the Solidarity Uprising.

Mom said I should already know about the Polish Solidarity movement, because my father was involved in it. (Thanks, Mom. I did know this about my father.) Mom also said, "Pop-yeh-woosh-ko" is spelled *Popieluszko*. There's a slanted stroke through the L which makes it pronounced like an English W.

Mary doesn't talk about politics much. She says she "hates" politics because it is only about "who is going to sit on the chair." Mostly she talks about her life in Poland and Canada. About her parents and brother and sisters. About her kids. About being a doctor.

While Mary talks, she also works. She's a perfectionist, and she thinks the Rec Plex should be as clean as a hospital. She makes sure I'm doing everything right. She tells me to check that the buckets, mops and rags are clean before I start and after I finish. She shows me how to hose the shower area, how to use the institutional washer and dryer, and so on.

My second day at work, when Mary covered for me because I was feeling sick, I realized that she is very kind. She is going to teach me how to sew fashionable clothes. And she doesn't just talk. She listens too. She must have been a good doctor and mother. She has three kids back in Poland. I think she already suspects I am depressed about the situation at home. Of course, I am also depressed because Curtis is ignoring me. Plus Sarah ignores me after school now too. Sarah has a new boyfriend who plays football and goes to the college.

It's not that I don't love Hanna. I do, even though she's definitely weird. I know she's always been there for Mom and me, even though I haven't seen her for the past four years. Hanna is sort of like a nun. She doesn't care about worldly things like clothes. Yet Hanna often disagrees with the Catholic Church. I guess Hanna is so intellectual that I can't understand her. I am not stupid, but I think reality is more important than ideas.

Anyway, for the past few years, Mom has been very worried about Hanna. Mom has been so obsessed about Hanna's strange behaviour, that she has been phoning her all the time, and going to Montreal to visit her, even when she had other things to do. Like work. And school. And take care of me. Mom kept saying: "Hanna is going to drown herself in the St. Lawrence River some day!"

Mom never neglected me or anything, but she stopped seeing our life objectively.

Since I got back at the beginning of September to Mapleville, life at our house has revolved around Hanna. I guess that's natural when someone is so sick, but it is depressing. Hanna doesn't make any demands. She says we don't have to visit her. She says she is content to lie in her room alone. But we can't forget about her. How can we? If you knew there was a wild animal under your porch suffering and dying, could you forget about it? And what if it was not a wild animal, but a pet you had loved for a long time?

Is life worth living? Good question. I wish I knew.

I like Mary because she is funny and fun. Sarah has these same qualities. But Sarah is different from Mary, because she is tall and beautiful, young and inexperienced. Also, Sarah is not interested in helping other people, while Mary is. Sarah is spoiled. Sarah thinks she will always get exactly what she wants. She's not snobbish, however, and I know she likes me. We always hang around together in school, even though I can't really talk to her, and even though she disappears after school. She says she "admires" me for getting a job to make my own money.

* * *

We had our Thanksgiving dinner tonight after I finished work. Joe ate at our house, because his boys are with their mother. Then he and Mom went over to his house to watch videos.

* * *

Mrs. Henderson, I'm very flattered that you like "The Blind Man's Song" so much. I will try setting it to music, like you suggested. You're the first teacher who has said I have writing talent. I guess I get that from my father's side of the family, although Mom says that her father also used to write poetry when he was young, and she did too.

I'm doing a big history project about Poland. I'm planning to send a copy of it to my father to impress him, so he'll invite me to come and see him. Mr. Dunlop said it doesn't matter that I don't have access to the Internet at home. He says the Internet is an unreliable source for research anyway, and he wants us to be able to use "primary and print" resources efficiently too.

Mom knows all about high tech stuff, but her own computer is fifteen years old. Mom says that she can't afford upgrades or Internet charges. She uses the college computers a lot.

I can do my history project easily by interviewing Mary. Mary talks frequently about Poland during the war and communism.

* * *

Here is what a Polish history book says about the beginning of World War II. The English version of this book is titled *History of Poland*. It was written by A. Gieysztor, and others, and published in Warsaw in 1979. It says: "The German attack on Poland began at dawn on September 1, 1939. Within a few weeks the Polish army, in spite of its heroic struggle, was defeated." The Polish nation experienced frightful "oppression and destruction" for almost six years under Nazi occupation.

Here is what the *History of Poland* says about how Polish people behaved during World War II: "There were no traitors in Poland during the Second World War. The Poles unanimously rejected Hitler's ultimatum of total destruction for their people and their country and were the first in Europe to offer him armed resistance.... The people tried to survive and despite everything dealt the enemy many a painful blow."

* * *

Joe came in last night when he brought Mom home. When I told him about the big history project I'm doing, he said he had the perfect title: "The Decline and Fall of the Soviet Empire, Or My Weird Life." I always feel like Joe is teasing me.

Curtis

I showed Mr. Speers, my old art teacher, my drawing of the woodpecker: "The Fallen Bird". He said I should definitely apply for art college. He said I have the talent to be any kind of artist I want. I could go into fine art or commercial art.

This morning at breakfast, when I told Mom what Mr. Speers said, she got all quiet. I could tell she's still worried that I'll turn out like Dad.

"Don't get your hopes up for art college unless you plan on paying for it yourself or getting into debt with loans," she said finally, instead of saying what she was really thinking.

"Dad has never missed a support payment, except when he was bankrupt," I reminded her. "Dad told me that he will back me financially on whatever I decide to do. Once his business is going well, he will help me through art school."

Mom didn't say anything more, but she frowned. Luckily, she had to go to work, and I had to go to school.

Otherwise we might have started arguing again.

After school I biked over to the pond behind the old power plant. The pond is full of garbage, but mallard ducks and Canada geese still flock there. So do trumpeter swans from the Wendake Wildlife Centre.

No sign of Steve. (Thumbs up.) No sign of She Wolf. (Thumbs down.)

Mom says I can't take her car for a weekend sketching trip to Point Pelee Park. The car supposedly needs repairs. Not true. She's just overly protective. Of me, not the car.

Meanwhile, I'm going to take a bus to Toronto to see some art galleries, like Mr. Speers suggested.

Mary

Miracles

One day during the war, as I am walking along the road, I hear the air raid sirens. I jump into the ditch, lie down, close my eyes and wait for the whines. The enemy airplanes fly in Vs like geese. Usually three planes, called "Stukas", fly together. As the Stukas swoop down, you hear a whine. As the bombs fall, you hear a whistle. As the bombs explode—boom!

But before I hear a whine, a voice inside my head says, "Not here!" So I jump out of the ditch, run into the field and throw myself down on the black earth. Just in time. Whine, whistle boom. Whine, whistle, boom. Whine, whistle, boom. Boom, boom, boom.

One bomb drops right where I had lain in the ditch! Boom! Dirt showers me like dry rain. There's a great big hole over there, but I am safe.

Another day, my brother gets into serious trouble. It's evening after dark, and Johnny is playing with matches near the forest on the bridge near our house. With a much older boy who should know better, Johnny lights match after match. The two boys drop the burning matches into the stream.

After my brother comes home, and we are getting ready for bed, Nazi soldiers burst into our house. They point their guns at us. Their leader orders us to stand against the wall.

"You are hiding Polish soldiers!" the leader says, pointing his gun at Mommy.

"No, we're not," says Mommy.

"We don't believe you," says the leader. "We saw their lights at the bridge near your house. They were signalling. We saw them."

"Honestly," says Mommy, standing against the wall with her hands in the air. "We are not hiding partisans. You can see for yourself."

The soldiers keep pointing their guns at us. Elizabeth and I start crying. Johnny remains silent and still, staring at the soldiers.

Then, for some reason, the soldiers decide that they believe Mommy, and they go away without even searching our house.

After they leave, my brother starts to giggle. Then he explains that it was he and his friend, not Polish soldiers, who had been lighting matches near the bridge.

Grandpa takes his belt out of his pants. He whips my brother hard! My brother nearly got us all killed!

Then, one day, we are really hungry. A bomb hit our potato field, and Nazi soldiers stole all our other food too. That day more Nazi soldiers come by, driving a herd of cows.

Grandpa knew the soldiers and cows were coming. A neighbour told him. Grandpa hobbled around as fast as he could, getting ready. Then he asked Mommy, Elizabeth, and Johnny to stay out of sight at the neighbours.

Grandpa leans on our gate as those enemy soldiers approach. He reaches inside his jacket, pulls out a small bottle, and uncorks it just as the soldiers go by with the herd of cows. He seems to take a drink from the bottle. I wonder what he's doing, because he's never done this before. Anyway, I can see his throat isn't moving, so he's only pretending to drink.

But I keep quiet and still, because he told me to. Grandpa picked me to come with him because I look so harmless. "Your mother is too angry, and Elizabeth is too beautiful, and Johnny is too mischievous," said Grandpa, "so you'll do for today."

As Grandpa is wiping his mouth and putting the bottle back inside his jacket, the leader of the soldiers comes up to him.

"Good day to you, sir!" says Grandpa very loudly in German. I know some words of German too, because now I hear that language almost every day. Grandpa understands lots of German words. He speaks the enemies' language almost as well as they do themselves.

Grandpa sounds very friendly when he speaks to the leader of the enemy soldiers. I think that is odd, because at home he doesn't sound at all friendly when he talks about the Nazis. But I keep quiet and still, because Grandpa told me to.

"Care for a drink?" Grandpa asks the leader. "Pure one hundred per cent Polish vodka. First class."

"Where did you get that?" asks the leader, yanking the bottle from Grandpa's hand. He's a big blonde man in a grey uniform.

"Bought it in the village," says Grandpa with a shrug. I know Grandpa isn't telling the truth, because I saw Grandpa filling the bottle this morning from a barrel he hid in the barn. But I keep quiet and still, like Grandpa told me to.

The cows don't keep quiet. They moo loudly, swat flies and make cow pies. They wish they were munching happily in a grassy field, instead of waiting hungrily on a dirt road.

"Good?" asks Grandpa as the leader takes a drink. "You can have the whole bottle."

"You know we'd take it anyway," says the leader, wiping his mouth and handing the bottle to another soldier.

Even though the leader shares the bottle with the other soldiers, he's not nice. He shoves Grandpa against the gate. Then he feels in all Grandpa's pockets for more bottles or for a gun.

"Sorry, can't help you," shrugs Grandpa. "No more vodka. No more nothing. But I tell you what."

"What, old man?" asks the leader.

"I see you need somebody to take care of your cows. I'll take care of them for you until you come back," says Grandpa. "I've got hay in my barn and a good big pasture. I can't feed people with hay and grass, but I can feed your cows, and I can milk them. I've got nothing else to do, and my granddaughter can help. Those cows look as though they need milking right now."

"How do you know we've been ordered away and need someone to take care of our cows?" asks the leader, shoving Grandpa against the gate again.

"I just guessed," shrugs Grandpa. "I see how hard you're driving those cows. Marching is not good for milk cows. You must be a city fellow, or you'd know that."

The leader lets Grandpa go.

"All right, old man," the leader says. "We'll leave the cows with you for a week, until we return. But they'd better be here when we get back, and they'd better be fattened up nicely on your hay and grass. Or else that scrawny little granddaughter of yours is chopped-up chicken feed."

And here the leader raises his pistol and aims it at my heart. I stay quiet and still, like Grandpa told me to.

Those enemy soldiers leave their herd of cows with Grandpa and me. There are almost thirty cows! Too many for just our little barn and pasture, so we share them with the whole village! One cow for every family!

Grandpa is the boss of the cows, and the whole village takes very good care of them. Not for a week, but for several months. And do you know how much milk, sour cream and butter you can get from thirty cows? Enough for a whole village!

The whole village shares bowls, pails and separators, as well as cows. A separator is a machine that divides the cream from the milk.

And do you know how much cheese you can make from so much milk? Enough for a whole village!

Grandpa makes huge rounds of Swiss cheese. He pours the liquid cheese into wooden forms. Then he hangs the forms for a long time to ripen. When the cheese is ripe, he puts wax around it.

In front of enemy soldiers, Grandpa pretends he is stupid, but he is not. He knows how to do lots of things.

The whole village eats that cheese all winter. And is it ever good!

Eva

The beginnings of the paralysis appeared last spring, in early June. By the time I arrived during the July 1st holiday, the little rented room was a sea of soiled tissue paper, half-eaten food, newspapers and clothing. Hanna's sinking ship was the narrow bed from which she rose only to shuffle to the sink, the hot plate, the washroom across the hall, or the convenience store across the street.

There had been no telephone for several months. She couldn't afford the expense. That's why I had not known. There had been no communication. She could not walk to the phone booth on the corner. Stamps were too expensive. Anyway, she had nothing to say.

White, fluffy, cottony bedding for seeds from the poplar tree outside the window had begun to pile up on the window sill and drift into the room. Insects had built a castle on the ripped screen that had been removed for repairs and left leaning against a wall.

I insisted that she see a doctor. Why? She knew she was going to die. She hadn't seen a doctor in four years, since the lump had risen in her breast. What was the use of fighting the disease? "Fighting the disease" is an absurd expression. Let death come. She was ready.

The world was too evil, she felt. She had lived through Nazism, communism and then capitalism. Any system could be evil if people made it so. Her two "adopted sons" had found no work. They had died. Now she wanted to die.

She herself had stopped looking for work when she realized how many young people were feeling hopeless because there were no decent jobs for them. The suicide statistics for young people in Quebec had mobilized her. After seeing the statistics, she set her pride aside and accepted welfare.

She had a plan.

The case worker at the welfare office was patronizing. He could not imagine how Hanna felt being forced to beg. Hanna was, after all, an art historian and librarian with years of professional experience. Furthermore, she had computer skills, language skills and practical skills. She'd taken every course available! She was willing to accept any job that wasn't illegal or immoral! She'd sew. She'd frame pictures. She'd wash dishes, scrub floors or pick fruit. She could not go on accepting financial help from me...even if that help barely kept her from starving on the street!

"You are over fifty years old, madame," says the case worker. "It is difficult to find work after forty. One is out of date. Then too you are a foreigner. Where are you from? Poland? You have been here only ten years. It is difficult for a foreigner to adjust to Canadian ways. One is out of step."

When the lump appeared, she was already a social activist. To herself she justified accepting welfare by actively contributing to the community. She worked with young people, especially students, teaching them to protest, teaching them that the system was wrong. One of her "adopted sons" was a poet. Another directed plays. She assured them that their activities were important.

"Expressing true feelings is important," she would tell them. "The single, dissenting voice is important. Pain is meaningful and must be described."

Hanna nursed her "adopted sons" as they died from AIDS. At the same time, she continued to help others: the dispossessed and betrayed. Eventually there was no division between herself and her vast, adopted family. For a while, she even lived among young drug addicts in a derelict building condemned for demolition. Strangely, no harm came to her. Or did it?

After both of her "sons" died, her heart seemed to burst from her chest. When I took her to the hospital, the doctor showed me how the lump in Hanna's breast had become a large open wound. The raw, diseased flesh looked like the heart itself emerging. Her own pain she had not described.

*   *   *

I found the following scribbled note in one of Hanna's boxes.

<u>Analysis of Canadian Society</u>
-Blockage of the circulation of information.
-Crude structure of society.
-Alienation and dispossession of a great part of the population.
-Socio-cultural underdevelopment and its consequences.
-Negative selection process (the misfits and socially unacceptable).
-Culture, art and literature exist apart from "real life." The essential role of these elements is not recognized, and society cannot develop harmoniously and structure itself organically.

* * *

I am looking forward to spending Saturday evening with Joe. I need to talk to him. I adore him. He is my rock.

Joe

A weekend to myself, except for an evening with Eva on Saturday. Eva showed me some of the handwritten notes she has found among Hanna's effects. She asked me if I thought Hanna was mentally ill.

I had to say, yes, at some point Hanna lost her sanity. Latterly, in Montreal, Hanna did crack. But I reminded Eva of the old dictum, "In much madness, sense."

I said that Hanna had shown "impressive courage" in her life choices.

I also said that I think Hanna is quite sane now.

"Love has restored her," I said. And Eva started crying.

I told Eva that she herself needed a few days of complete rest. Then we watched some videos Eva wanted to see: two French Canadian films called *The Decline and Fall of the American Empire*, and *Jesus of Montreal*. They had English subtitles.

Eva and I agreed that the films validate some of Hanna's criticisms of Quebec society, and North American society.

Before I took Eva home, I brewed her a pot of herbal tea to help her get a good night's sleep.

I drove aimlessly around the countryside Sunday afternoon, missing Eva, who spent a much needed day in bed. The boys have gone with Jill to visit her parents. I got some decent shots of a front moving through.

Sunday evening I went through my unread book collection and spent a few hours with Joseph Campbell's *Hero with a Thousand Faces*. Marked assignments Monday.

Week Six

Naomi

Saturday, October 16, 1999

I have been mopping this floor endlessly. I have mopped the entire area around the key desk, the entrance in front of the main reception desk, and the halls between. The mop is enormous. The bucket is enormous. My arms are hurting. My back is hurting. I'm almost finished mopping. Suddenly some kids from my school thunder past like a herd of retro Mickey Mouse Club rejects, tramping mud on my clean floor.

"Didn't you see the sign?" I say.

"What sign?" says Melony Price.

"Wet Floor," I say.

"So sorry, darling," Melony says, "but we have to walk somewhere. Now don't go and tell Mr. Dunlop on me."

I don't say anything. I just gape.

Melony brays to the herd: "She's an incredible brown noser! You should see the way she sucks up to our history teacher! The poor thing is in love with an old man!"

When they enter the women's locker room, I leave the mop and bucket in the middle of the floor and run to the staff room. Mary is there. When she looks at me, I start to cry.

I sit on the sofa and cry for a long time. Mary sits beside me in a chair waiting silently and watching me with her all-seeing, dark-grey eyes. Then I tell her about the past four years, about Hanna going crazy and my mother always being like a teacher with me and like a panicking kid with Hanna. Mary listens carefully, and when I finish she makes me a mug of hot chocolate and tells me she will visit our house.

Mary thinks maybe she knows my mother and Hanna from a long time ago in Poland. Anyway, she'd like to talk to somebody besides me and her landlady. Mary didn't go anywhere for Thanksgiving last weekend. I feel awful that I didn't ask her to come to our house for dinner on Saturday. But she probably wouldn't have come anyway. She had dinner by herself, and then she went to church. She couldn't go to church on Sunday morning, because she was working.

*   *   *

Mary came for dinner this evening. I knew it was okay to invite her without letting Mom know ahead of time. On Saturday, Mom always tidies our place and cooks a special meal for Joe and me. I'm always allowed to invite someone to join us, but I usually don't. I thought about inviting Sarah, but I didn't want her to see how crowded our house is, or how strange Hanna is. Sarah wouldn't understand. She would be shocked if she saw

76

how our living room is filled with boxes of documents from Hanna's room in Montreal.

The documents are reports, pamphlets and newspaper clippings. They are also Hanna's notes from meetings of the Civil Liberties Association, Native rights groups, students' rights groups, gay and lesbian rights' groups, AIDS victim groups, unemployed groups and anti-poverty groups. The boxes aren't labelled; Mom has not organized them yet. There are also some placards. They are leaning against the living room walls. Here is a sample, translated by me from French: "WE, THE UNEMPLOYED, ARE DEMONSTRATING IN GREAT NUMBERS. WE ARE PROTESTING AGAINST CUTS TO UNEMPLOYMENT INSURANCE! IT IS NECESSARY TO FIGHT UNEMPLOYMENT, NOT THE VICTIMS OF UNEMPLOYMENT!"

The woman was obsessed! The only thing Hanna didn't protest about was Quebec separating from the rest of Canada. Mom says that shows Hanna's "independence of thought", because Hanna didn't think about what everybody else was thinking about. I myself think about global warming sometimes, but I know it's inevitable. It's just going to happen. I can't do anything about it.

Mary and I finished work at four-thirty p.m. Then Mary went home, had a shower and changed into a pretty, sky-blue dress. Then, on her way to my house, she bought a bouquet of red and white carnations for Hanna (red and white are Poland's colours), and a box of chocolates for Mom. Mary shook hands with Hanna, Mom and Joe. Then she chatted cheerfully in her awful English. Soon everyone was chatting cheerfully and even laughing.

Mary knows how to make people relax. Also, by amazing coincidence, Hanna was a patient of Mary's long ago. They remembered each other well.

At the dinner table, Mary, Mom, Joe and I talked about all kinds of topics like the weather, teaching, truck driving, cleaning, the NATO bombing of Yugoslavia last spring, the Kosovar refugees coming to Canada, the Pope's (fourth? fifth?) visit to Poland last June, Mary's children and grandchildren, and Anne Murray's daughter getting anorexia but recovering. We even discussed the fact that in the nineteenth century there used to be a stop on the Underground Railway right here in Mapleville, and local people hid runaway slaves.

Mary, Mom, Joe and I did all this talking at the kitchen table. This is our only table, because our house is too small for a dining room. Then Mary visited with Hanna, while I did the dishes, and Mom and Joe went to a "long, relaxing" movie. Would you believe *Star Wars Episode One: The Phantom Menace*? I thought that was for kids! Mom said the movie was too "violent," but otherwise "fun."

Hanna was amazingly talkative while Mary was with her. I could hardly believe how much Hanna said to Mary. And I am sure Hanna had a really nice evening. Mary didn't talk about anything medical or depressing with Hanna, she just treated her like a normal person and told her stories about her own life now and back in Poland, as she always does.

Mom's doctor just barged in last Wednesday, unannounced, in the middle of our dinner, about two weeks after the nurse asked him to come. He just marched in and started talking to Hanna about euthanasia.

"Theoretically, you can end your life any time by swallowing a bottle of morphine tablets," the doctor said. "But I can't authorize that. I understand your philosophy, but the law is the law." The doctor spoke English too quickly for Hanna to understand. Then he got impatient when he felt that Mom took too long translating what he had said into French. He left after only about ten minutes. Mom was furious with him.

Curtis

Got a job at a supermarket to earn money for a car. Dad said on the phone that he will help if I earn half myself.

So far, Steve is still staying away from us, and Mom is still depressed. It's good that Mom and I are so busy right now. We can avoid each other.

No time to draw or paint this weekend. No time for anything except work and school. Dad didn't have much time to talk on the phone. He's got a big new contract.

Some of the guys who work at the supermarket are morons. All they talk about is how much they drank, how many times they've had sex, and how fast they drove their car.

Luckily, I am an excellent liar.

Life sucks.

Mr. Speers said I should try to do well in my academic subjects, not just barely pass. He says he thinks I might be able get a scholarship for art college.

Sketched stuffed birds last weekend. On Saturday, it was raining by the time I got almost as far as the park on my bike, so I went into the museum. By the time I finished, the sun had come out again. A lot of species from around this area are already extinct. I did a pretty good passenger pigeon.

Started a cartoon strip called, "Nothing."
In the story nothing happens, so I draw nothing.
The cartoon strip is hilarious.
Hardy-har-har.

Mary

The Water Closet

One evening during the war there comes a quiet tap, tap, tap on our door. To open your door after dark is dangerous. Many people never do. But Mommy opens the door.

"Can you hide us in your house?" whispers a shadow.

"Come in quickly," says Mommy, wiping her hands on her apron.

Six men. Jews! We know them by the yellow stars on their shirts. Nazi soldiers are rounding them up like cattle, shooting them, or sending them to death camps. These Jews are good people. They are our neighbours. When I was a little kid, I went to school with their little kids.

Some Catholic kids said matzo bread is made of gentile flesh rolled around in barrels with nails sticking through, so all the blood runs out. But Mommy said matzo bread is just dry flat bread, so I tried it, and it tasted good. In religion class I visited the synagogue once. It was interesting.

Anyway, it isn't only the Jews they are sending away. It is Christians like us, too. Everybody the Nazis want to get rid of. Priests, teachers. Anybody who can fight them.

"I'll hide you in the water closet," says Mommy. "Maybe the soldiers won't look there."

The Jews follow Mommy to the very farthest, far back part of the house. One moment, and those six grown men all squeeze somehow into the water closet.

A water closet is a tiny room with just a toilet. No bathtub. Not even a sink to wash your hands. Really like a closet or a phone booth. It is small even to me alone, and I am just one little girl.

"Not a sound. Not a movement," says Mommy to the poor frightened men. "If the soldiers find you, they will shoot us too."

"We know," say the Jews. "God bless you."

Mommy shuts the door of the water closet. Then she leads us children back to the living room where we have been playing.

She kisses Johnny and me and tells us to go on playing. (My sister Elizabeth is not home. She has gone with Grandpa to do something.)

"Say nothing about this," Mommy warns us. "Act as though nothing has happened."

"We understand," say Johnny and I.

I go on playing with the big doll my aunt brought me from Krakow long ago, before the war. I cut her open to see what is inside, and then I sew her up, like Mommy sews up wounded people. Johnny opens up the old clock that doesn't work any more, and then he puts it back together again. He is like Grandpa and

Daddy, my brother. He knows how to fix machines.

Soon there comes a bang, bang, bang on our door. Mommy opens the door, and Nazi soldiers barge into the house. Big blonde men in grey uniforms, with guns and dirty boots.

Johnny and I do not move or speak.

"Where are the Jews?" demand the soldiers, rushing into the house. "Where have you hidden them?"

"There are no Jews here," says Mommy. "I am making supper, and my children are playing quietly. We are alone here. See for yourself."

The enemy soldiers begin to search from room to room. They step on our rugs in their dirty boots. They yank open our doors and drawers. They throw down or knock over our things. Crash! Crash!

Will they look in the water closet?

Mommy stands icy-still under the picture of the Virgin Mary. Even though she isn't moving her lips, I know she is praying

I go on sewing my doll. My brother goes on fixing the clock. Johnny and I are very careful. We put things back the way we find them. We like everything to be just so.

The Nazi soldiers are not careful. They overturn furniture and don't put it back. They empty cupboards and leave our clothes lying in messy heaps. They leave dirt on Mommy's nice clean floors.

It seems like the soldiers are searching for hours.

They search every room in our house. They search everywhere.

Except the water closet.

Then, finally, the soldiers are gone. And they haven't found the Jews!

The soldiers have left the front door open. Johnny gets up and closes it quietly. Mommy kneels in front of the Virgin Mary. Now she is praying out loud. I run to the door of the water closet.

"The soldiers are gone," I whisper. "But don't come out yet, because they might come back."

When Grandpa and Elizabeth return after dark, Grandpa tells my brother to fetch some of Daddy's clean white shirts.

Then Grandpa opens the door to the water closet. He tells the Jews to come out. He tells them to take off their shirts with the yellow stars.

Grandpa burns the shirts of the Jewish men in our stove. Then, after the Jews put on Daddy's shirts, Mommy and I give them some supper to take with them. Their supper is cheese and bread that we have tied up in clean rags.

Then the Jews are gone.

"They've gone to somewhere safe in the forest," Grandpa says.

Clothes and food are pretty scarce during the war. But we aren't the only people who help others. Many people leave food on the edge of the forest and in the cemeteries. This food is for Jews and partisans who are hiding, cold, hungry and afraid.

The partisans are a kind of Polish soldier. Daddy is a soldier. He is away somewhere fighting the Nazis. We don't know where.

Yes, people help other people. At least, some people do. I hear the grownups talking about it.

One night after curfew, a woman runs through the village with her baby in her arms. The baby is sick.

The woman is so worried about her baby, that she forgets about the curfew. She forgets that the Nazis shoot you dead, no questions asked, if they see you on the street after a certain time.

That woman is a Catholic, like us. But it is Jews who save her. The Jews pull that woman and her baby inside their house, before the soldiers see them.

Eva

I should listen to Naomi more. I don't give her enough credit for her good sense. She is maturing rapidly, and she is intelligent in different ways from Hanna and me. Whereas Hanna and I are logical, Naomi is intuitive. Naomi sensed Doctor Kowalska's wisdom and brought her here to help. Yet she just thinks of Doctor Kowalska as a new friend, as "Mary."

Hanna is relieved to have her own doctor here. She enjoys talking to a fellow countrywoman in her native language.

It's not merely that Doctor Kowalska is familiar and Polish. She also understands what Hanna has gone through here. Both women are brilliant professionals who have been forced to do menial labour in Canada. Both have been plunged from the top to the bottom of society. Both feel powerless, yet both have much to offer. They see so much. They have so much to say, so much wisdom that mainstream Canadians could learn from. Yet they are marginalized.

Dr. Kowalska says she'll come and visit Hanna as often as she can. She says she'll bring her some Polish dishes to eat. And a Warsaw newspaper from a Polish shop in Mapleville that I didn't even know about. And she'll chat with Hanna. I am so relieved. Hanna has been asking for dishes that I don't know how to make. The other day it was *kasza*. I had some buckwheat that I'd bought in a health food store, so I boiled it up. But Hanna couldn't eat it. Then, when I tried to cook potato pancakes, Hanna couldn't eat those either. (Dr. K. says the cancer may already have spread to Hanna's stomach and brain.)

Hanna never cared about traditional Polish food before now. When we were together, we took turns cooking the simplest things, like scrambled eggs. Anything quick, inexpensive and nutritious. Mind, heart and soul were more important than body.

* * *

Here is another of Hanna's scribbled notes. It was in one of the boxes. It is undated. I find it harrowing.

I looked at my watch: ten minutes past eleven. It began to rain a bit. I walked quickly from the _____ subway station north on _____ Street.

In front of the entrance of _____ where the Ministry of Health and Social Services is located, a group of people formed a circle; the placards moved in a ring.

I began to understand the slogans. Among others: "They talk and we die."

A knife stroke in my heart.

For me it was not a slogan.

I know well what that means.

Joe

Took Eva and the boys to see *Star Wars*. We didn't tell Naomi we were taking Jeff and Jerry. I think Eva is too sensitive about Naomi's feelings.

But what do I know about teenage girls?

Eva didn't try to get close to the boys. She spoke to them politely, almost as though they were adults.

Eva thinks I'm "great" with Naomi. Evidently Naomi does not agree. Nevertheless, I seem to perceive that Naomi is becoming slightly less hostile.

But I'm probably wrong.

At least the boys like me. Had a great day with them Sunday. No time for my photography, only for their hockey and homework. Big expedition to the library.

Is my growing cynicism about teaching part of the proverbial mid-life crisis? No, I really need more freedom and creativity.

On the other hand, it would be terrible to be without a decent pension in ten years, like this Polish doctor. She's cleaning floors. Where's the freedom in that?

I guess I just have to hang on for a while yet. At least I feel needed. Occasionally.

Eva's got herself involved in some committee looking into purchasing new industrial robots for the technology department at the college. She has an amazing capacity for hard work and for compartmentalizing her life.

But she needs a hobby—something to relax with and regain perspective.

Week Seven

Naomi

Sunday, October 24, 1999

Today I spent eight hours at the Rec Plex, working with Mary. It's amazing how little I knew about her, when I thought I knew a lot. Mary told me that she is all alone here in Canada, because her older brother and sister are dead. Mary stays here because she can earn more money with minimum-wage jobs in Canada than she can earn with a doctor's job in Poland. If she stays, she can help her kids financially.

She says she had three grandchildren when she left Poland, and now she has five.

"Two of them I have never held in my arms!" she says. She says she hasn't seen any of her children or grandchildren for eight years.

"How can I afford to go to Poland?" she says. "I am starting from zero, just like my Daddy did after First World War, just like my Grandpa did after Second World War."

Mary is working three jobs. As well as cleaning, she sews and babysits.

"Even with three jobs," she says, "I have barely enough to live on, because I must help my children."

I told Mary that my Great-grandmother Goralski worked as a cleaner at the University of Alberta for fifteen years. Great-grandma Goralski saved up enough money for my mother to study at university. But then, after my mother graduated from engineering, she had trouble finding a job in her field, because she was a woman with a small child.

Mary has lots of problems, but she doesn't get as depressed about them as Hanna did. Maybe this is because Mary has religious faith and goes to church all the time. Or because she has children and grandchildren she has to help. Or because she trusts capitalism more. Or because she trusts people more.

Mary and I didn't talk just about our problems. We talked about travel, education, medicine and fashion, as well as sewing. We're going to borrow her landlady's sewing machine this evening, and Mary's going to give me my first sewing lesson. Mom and Hanna are silent mostly, but Mary is almost never silent. Her stories bubble up like a spring of pure water. She tells hundreds of stories that all flow into each other. Her stories have endings, yet they never end. Maybe she does this because she is a doctor. Maybe she uses stories to help cure people.

* * *

This is a few days later: Wednesday, October 27. I know I'm supposed to write my diary entry at one sitting, but I didn't have much to write about before, and now I've got lots. Today Sarah invited me to her house for the first time. She invited me to eat dinner and study for our biology test. I was delighted that Sarah had time to visit with me after school, and I was eager to see the inside of Sarah's gorgeous house and get to know her better. Furthermore, I wanted to go say something to Curtis, who lives near Sarah.

Curtis does live on the same block as Sarah, but he does not live in a big, beautiful, new house like Sarah's. Instead, he lives in a small, ugly, old house like ours. Curtis told me on the plane that his parents are divorced, and that his dad lives in Edmonton. I guess his dad doesn't send much support money, and his mother doesn't make much money working as a secretary.

When I knocked on Curtis's front door, I started worrying that he would think that the clothes I was wearing were too expensive and showy. I was ready to walk away and pretend I had rung the wrong doorbell by mistake, when the door opened. And there he was.

"Um, hi, Curtis!" I say.

"Hi!" Curtis says. "You're the girl from the plane, aren't you?" He looks sort of tired and rumpled. His hair needs trimming, and his Tyrannosaurus rex sweatshirt is faded and wrinkled. But I think he looks great.

"Yes, I am, and my name is Naomi," I say. "Look, I'm sorry to bother you, but I just happened to be in the neighbourhood, and I have a message for you." *(Dummy! How can you use that trite phrase, "happened to be in the neighbourhood"? Now he'll know for sure that you are a total idiot!)*

"So, how are you doing?" Curtis says. "Sorry I

didn't call, but I've been very busy with my art work and school."

"Why didn't you speak to me when you passed me in the hall the other day." I blurt. *(You were not going to mention that! Not! Not!)*

"Passed you in the hall?" he says. "I didn't even see you. Sorry."

(How come I know he is lying?)

"That's okay. It doesn't matter," I lie. "Probably a case of mistaken identity. Anyway, the message is from the aquatic director of the Recreation Complex—that's where I work. She says she needs a mural painted on the walls around the shallow pool, where the little kids learn to swim. I happened to be, uh, cleaning in her office when she mentioned this. I told her you draw great animal pictures, especially birds. She says she'll pay you. The kids are really young, so the pictures can't be scary, but otherwise you could probably paint whatever you want. Maybe you could just phone her and talk to her. You could recommend another artist if you don't want the job."

"Okay, sure, Naomi. Thanks," says Curtis. "Can you give me her name and number? I'll call her tomorrow."

I hand Curtis the piece of paper the aquatic director gave me. Then I notice that he is looking sort of uncomfortable, so I just mumble, "Hope she pays you a lot. I've got to go now. Bye."

"Bye…and thanks," says Curtis closing the door as I run down the sidewalk.

He doesn't even care if he never sees me again! He doesn't even care! I yell silently at myself, as I run towards Sarah's place. *How could I have been so dumb?*

* * *

When I got to Sarah's, I didn't tell her anything about what happened at Curtis's. I can't talk to Sarah about things that are important to me. I don't know why. I mean, Sarah is really nice, but she's too confident, and too beautiful and a really good singer. I guess I'm a coward. I think she'd drop me if she knew what my life was really like. When I'm around her, I prefer to be just sort of a mirror for her. I agree with everything she says and act like a groupie. It's disgusting.

At least I saw the inside of her gorgeous house. I also found out a little about her life, which can't be as perfect as I thought. Sarah's father, mother and brother did not say one word to each other at dinner. Later, while Sarah and I were upstairs, sitting in her spacious and tastefully decorated bedroom, Sarah's parents and brother were downstairs yelling at each other. Her brother yelled that her father is having an affair with his secretary. Her father yelled that her brother is doing drugs. Her mother yelled that she didn't want to hear about any of this. Her father yelled back that her mother is a "religious fanatic." Her brother yelled at her father not to yell at her mother.

I felt really uncomfortable hearing all this. Sarah said she thought she would probably run away to Paris or New York before the school year is finished. Sarah also admitted that she had actually invited me over because her boyfriend was at an out-of-town football game. She explained that she needed to talk to somebody about her family's problems, because she was going crazy. We talked so much about Sarah's family's problems, that we didn't study.

On my way home from Sarah's, I felt angry with Sarah for inviting me under false pretenses and making me fail the biology test. I also felt angry with myself for picking friends who don't care about me. I suddenly wondered: *Does anybody care about anybody?* Then I felt totally depressed. When I got home, I phoned Mary and told her how I felt.

Mary said I should play some music: "Something for your Mom and Hanna. Something soft that makes heart feel good." So I did. I went to the piano and played some of my old classical pieces, like the Chopin waltz and Beethoven's "Moonlight Sonata". Then I played some of Mom's favourites, like Anne Murray's "Snow Bird" and Rita MacNeil's "Flyin' on Your Own". I didn't make fun of these songs, like I usually do. Then I played and sang "Hangin' by a Thread".

I feel better now.

Curtis

I'm working on a physics assignment due the next morning when the doorbell rings. I peek out the window to see if it's Steve, but it's She Wolf.

I want to pretend I'm not home, but by then she's seen me, so I answer the door.

She is as beautiful as ever. She says that she is working as a cleaner, but I find this statement difficult to believe, because her clothes look too expensive. She also says that the Mapleville Recreation Complex is looking for an artist to paint a mural.

I act totally stupid. She gives me the Rec Plex

telephone number. I don't even invite her to come in.

Then, after she leaves, I rip up the number and throw it in the garbage.

Why did I do that?

Why am I a gutless freak? Why am I scared of a beautiful girl? Why did I turn down my first paying commission? Because I didn't get it myself? Because it came from a girl?

For a while I lay on my bed, staring at the ceiling.

I wanted to die. I kept imagining myself some big war hero getting shot in action.

Then I fell asleep without finishing the physics assignment.

What an idiot! What a gutless idiot!

Mr. Bell just gave me a hard look when I said I didn't have the assignment ready because I had to work late at my part-time job. Then he said to get the assignment under his door before the next morning, or else. I copied from Tom at lunch and slid the assignment under Bell's door after school. Bell will probably figure out what I did.

What a freaking, gutless, lying, cheating idiot!

I am not worthy of the animal kingdom.

Mary

The Baby in the Blanket

Many days and nights there is a loud and terrible sound. The air raid siren. When the siren wails, everyone is supposed to run for the underground shelter, if they can.

The shelter is like a big basement. All the neighbours

hide down there when the enemy airplanes drop bombs.

Anyway, one neighbour who usually runs with us is a young woman. She is a friend of Agnes, my grown-up sister. When the siren wails, this young woman carries her baby in a blanket as she runs.

Another neighbour is an old woman—a grandmother like I am now. When the siren wails, the old woman carries a suitcase as she runs. And she runs away from the shelter, towards our house! She always does this!

"Madame, you're running the wrong way!" shouts my brother.

But the silly granny ignores his warning and keeps on running the wrong way.

She thinks she will be safe in our house, which is big and strong, but she is wrong. No house is safe from the bombs. We know people who were killed in their pyjamas in their beds. They didn't hear the siren and went on sleeping.

Anyway, the planes are coming closer. We can hear their terrible roar.

Down into the shelter we run. Down under the ground to be safe from the bombs.

Then we are sitting with our neighbours in the dark shelter. We are listening to the thud, thud, thud of the bombs exploding. We are safe, but what will happen to the old woman up above? What will we see when the airplanes are gone, and we return to our house? Maybe we won't even have a house.

Suddenly in the dark beside us, the young woman with the baby in the blanket screams.

"My baby!" she screams. "It's not here! The blanket

is empty! I dropped my baby! My baby! My baby! My baby!"

The young woman screams and screams.

"Hush!" say the neighbours. "Please be quiet, madame."

"Hush!" says Mommy taking the young woman in her arms. "There's nothing to be done."

Finally the whining of the planes and the thudding of the bombs are finished. We can go home, if we have a home.

Mommy keeps one arm tightly around the young woman, who can hardly walk. Grandpa takes me firmly by one hand and Elizabeth firmly by the other hand. Johnny walks behind Mommy, and we walk behind him. Slowly, we mount the steps.

What waits above? Fire, fire all around. Heaps of broken cement and bricks where a building stood. A man with his arms and legs blown away. He is still alive. His head and trunk are flip-flopping like a mechanical toy.

You think we children never see such things? Ha! We see plenty! We even see other children blown up. Sometimes there are landmines. Sometimes they are in the shape of a can, or a bar of soap, or a doll lying on the road. Of course, children will kick or pick up such things without thinking. Then, boom! There is nothing left of that child except bloody pieces.

Anyway, Grandpa puts his arms around Elizabeth and me. He holds us tightly. My brother bolts ahead. He does not listen when Mommy shouts, "No, Johnny! Come back!"

I close my eyes. I let Grandpa lead me along.

Grandpa is almost carrying me, even though I am walking. I have seen enough.

"Look!" Johnny shouts. "Our house is still here! The old woman is all right, and so is the baby!"

I lean into Grandpa. I stay under his arm. He keeps holding me tightly.

But I open my eyes to look.

The old woman is sitting on our doorstep. She is cradling the baby in her arms. The old woman and baby are completely unharmed! Not a bruise or a scratch!

The young woman snatches her baby. She clutches it closely. It begins to cry.

"No harm done," says the old woman cheerfully. "The baby is hungry. That's all."

And Mommy, Grandpa, Johnny and I, and all the neighbours who have gathered around, begin to laugh. We laugh and laugh.

Elizabeth doesn't laugh. She is always serious these days. She just stands there and watches the rest of us laugh. Mommy sees this. Mommy goes and puts her arms around Elizabeth.

Then Johnny asks the old woman: "Madame, why do you always run the wrong way with your suitcase? What's in the suitcase? Clothing? Documents? Gold?"

"There's nothing in the suitcase," replies the old woman, flinging it open for all to see.

And Mommy, Grandpa, my brother, and I, and all the neighbours, laugh some more.

And so it goes, the war. Sometimes I see the night sky lit up like a Christmas tree, with explosions and fire. Once I see a dog with a medicine bag strapped to its back, crawling on its belly under the bullets to reach a wounded man. The man takes a bandage from the medicine bag, and then the dog crawls away.

My Daddy and all of my uncles—Mommy's big, strong brothers—were killed in that terrible World War. They died in battles far away from home. They died in France. In Africa. But somehow, Mommy, Grandpa, my brother, my sisters and I survived.

Still, we too lost our home.

Eva

As Hanna lies dying in my house, hundreds of kilometres from her little rented room in the centre of Montreal, she watches the play of light and shadows on the wall. I watch too, when I can, in a few snatched moments of companionable silence. Sometimes the light is still. The light looks like veins on the back of a hand, or rivers seen from far above, seen by a bird or a mountain goat. Sometimes the shadows stream like water or flame. Sometimes the shadows are still. The shadows look like a huge rough cross, or like the ears of a small animal watching from a corner.

Watching the play of light and shadows, Hanna says she remembers her childhood in Poland. In this clean and pleasant room, with green plants, she begins to remember the good things. It is quiet here, without the constant ambulance and police sirens of a big city. She can even hear birds. Without moving her head, or leaving her bed, she can also watch the trees outside the window. The trees turn from green, to red and yellow, to black and white.

There is nothing more for doctors to do, except to

ease the pain with drugs. My English Canadian doctor provides the little pills. Hanna takes the weakest dosage possible. She has not taken a single one of the morphine pills the doctor prescribed.

She prefers agonizing pain to a mind unclear.

I am afraid she might take a whole bottle of morphine pills, so I do not leave the bottle within her reach.

Am I cowardly? Rationally, I agree with Hanna that, if one is of sound mind, one should be able to choose when and how to end one's own life. Yet I do not want to be accused of murder. And I might be so accused, if I left a bottle of morphine pills near her, and she swallowed them all. Furthermore, I am emotionally unable to accept Hanna's argument that she should die now, so as not to be a further burden on me, so as to die with dignity. I am afraid that she is still alive for some divine reason.

As well as watching the wall, Hanna watches the door. The door is where people come from. Naomi and I come a few times a day, and a nurse comes once a day. The nurses wash her, or massage her feet, or change the bedding, or talk to me. Many days I need more help than Hanna does. I am distraught about Hanna wanting to die. I think I have been distraught in varying degrees for several years.

The nurses are of many nationalities, but none are Polish. All speak English well. Many understand the unusual situation in this home turned hospice.

"She does not want to live any longer," I say to a nurse. "She says this treatment is inhumane. She does not want to become more and more helpless. She believes in euthanasia. She pleaded with the doctor to end her life quickly. Of course, he said he couldn't do it."

Hanna says she wants to die, yet when the doctor in Montreal told her she would die within a few months, her face wilted like a flower in a sudden frost.

If you were awake in the night when the frost came, and if you could see in the dark, you would see what her face looked like.

"She turned her back on life several years ago," I explain to the nurse. "She lost the will to live when she lost so many people she loved. The same thing happened to her mother. Her mother died at the same age and for the same reason—a broken heart."

She likes to lie alone in her room. When someone comes to her room, she searches the face. What does she search for? Understanding? Love? Her eyes look like the ethereal essence of six million flowers, so delicate is their expression.

What does she find on the faces? In the other eyes? Fear? Anger? Arrogance? Confusion? Boredom? All the things that people feel. Other people's feelings press upon her. People—the doctor, the nurses, the hospice volunteers, a sister and a niece—are so needy. They need so much from her. She needs nothing from them.

She is like a blessed relic, this wreck of a human being. Each person who encounters her receives from her a true mirror of himself or herself. Receives what he or she needs to learn. The sister is steadied, the niece is teased gently, a nurse is encouraged.

Are all the dying so helpful in their helplessness? Certainly not all of them can be as extraordinarily strong in spirit as Hanna.

I told Joe once that I feel as though I am witnessing

a slow crucifixion. He said that the same notion has occurred to him. He's going to look up a poem by W.H. Auden he once read. The poem is about how, as Christ was crucified, dogs went on living their "doggy lives."

Joe is astoundingly well read in the humanities. Yet he is never pedantic. He says he's a "seeker." I could not have a more thoughtful, loving, dear companion.

I believe that Hanna's life has enormous significance. I feel as though I should get the details down, in case, like the apostles, I let decades pass before I write down the whole story. I am a most inadequate apostle.

Joe

Must reread W.H. Auden. I promised Eva that I would find one particular poem of his, but I could not find it in my anthology of modern verse. I'll have to borrow his collected poems from the library. I did find Auden's "September 1, 1939". Liked it just as much as ever.

I have been immersed in a book John Van der V. loaned me: *Quiet Heroes: True Stories of the Rescue of Jews by Christians in Nazi-Occupied Holland.*

The book is by a Jewish-Canadian psychiatrist, André Stein. Stein interviewed some of the few Dutch people who assisted Jews during World War II. Most Dutch people did not assist. Most of Holland's Jews died.

Stein seems to find little that distinguishes those who helped from those who did not.

I wish I could ask my father whether our family hid Jews. What's the use of being half Dutch if I know little about Dutch culture and history?

Eva says I should go to Holland for a visit. Going to

Poland changed her life, she says. I'd like to go to my grandparents' village.

I asked Eva if she'd go with me. She got vague and said, "Maybe later."

I told her Naomi's never going to fully accept me, and that's that. Naomi is waiting for her knight-in-shining-armour father.

Eva got upset and pleaded with me not to be angry. She said she can't choose me over her daughter and dying sister. Of course, I told her I understand. And I do.

There are some advantages to being the fifty-something veteran of two failed marriages and a victorious battle with the bottle.

Eva threw her arms around me like I was some kind of hero.

Sometimes I think it is easier to be a true hero in war time. Selfless acts are wrung from you, because the circumstances are extraordinary.

Those of us who have known only peace easily degenerate into idle wilfulness. We consider ourselves first. We do not accept the existence of higher moral imperatives.

Unless, of course, we're religious.

Week Eight

Naomi

Saturday, October 30, 1999

When I went to work this morning, I was excited about designing an outfit for my singing act. I finally told Sarah that I love to sing and play music, and she invited me to audition for her band. Her band needs an extra act for a Christmas gig they're doing. Mary and I were going to make a pattern for my outfit tonight after work. Mary was going to come for dinner at my place, visit with Hanna and help me with the pattern.

I've had two lessons on Mary's landlady's sewing machine, and I'm going to buy my own second-hand sewing machine when I save enough money. I'm making so little money with this job, I'll never save up enough to go somewhere warm at Christmas anyway. And who would I go with? Sarah's family is supposedly going to Florida, but I don't want to go with them and listen to their arguing. Besides, they haven't invited me. Anyway, they might not go now.

As it turned out, Mary and I didn't make the

pattern for my outfit. Mary was very tired and upset. She just wanted to go to her room and rest after work. Then she wanted to go to the Saturday-evening mass.

The new, young director of the Rec Plex hired two men to clean full time at night. Then the director reduced Mary and the other full-time, day-time woman cleaner to part-time. The women are supposed to work about three-quarters time. But they still have to do the same amount of work as before! And they no longer receive benefits like dental insurance or sick leave!

The director says that Mary and the other woman will do less work. He says that he has "reorganized" the work. But Mary says that the director does not know what the work is really like. She says the director never consulted her. He only did calculations on paper. I suspect that the director did not consult Mary, because he could not understand her English. The director probably doesn't know Mary was a doctor. He doesn't seem to notice that she does a super job of cleaning.

I told Mary that I would quit my job in protest of this obvious discrimination against women, and that she should quit too. She said I shouldn't quit, because this is my first job ever104 and good experience. She said she's not quitting because she won't be able to find another job.

*   *   *

To show Mary that I care about what happens to her, I walked over to her place after supper and went with her to her church. I have never been to a Catholic mass before. Mom always says that I should make up my own mind about religion. She feels that the quarter of me that is Jewish is very important, but so are the three-quarters that are Catholic.

Mom admires the Polish pope, and she is proud of the Catholic tradition, but she disagrees with the church about a lot of things, like divorce. She is also skeptical about the Virgin birth, which she says is a myth. But she says that myth is not necessarily bad.

Mom and Joe watched a TV series where an American journalist named Bill Moyers interviewed a professor named Joseph Campbell. Campbell writes books about myth. Mom and Joe had long discussions at the dinner table about how myth should not mean "lie", as it does so often in modern society, but another way of seeing the truth.

Joe said: "Myth is an effective way of encoding truth in so-called primitive societies." Whatever that's supposed to mean.

Mary doesn't *discuss* her religion. She really *believes* it. Yet she knows a lot about modern science because she is a doctor. While she was kneeling, praying, singing and going up to the front for communion, I was sitting in the pew beside her. I did not move or make a sound; I only watched. The most interesting thing for me was the procession at the beginning and end of the mass, when the priests entered and exited carrying this huge cross that could be seen above the assembled worshippers. The procession with the cross was eerie and beautiful. It was like time travelling, like journeying back through centuries of Christianity.

I think Mary really *believes* because of everything

she has been through, and everything she is still going through. She also believes because, as a doctor, she knows that faith, even more than music, helps in hard times.

*   *   *

Here is what *Poland: A Tourist Guide* said about the Warsaw Uprising: "The Warsaw Uprising broke out on August 1, 1944, and continued 63 days, every underground organization in the city joining in the battle. Some 22,000 underground soldiers and 180,000 civilians were killed. Afterwards, the Nazis deported all the remaining population and proceeded with the systematic destruction of the city." Those were truly hard times for the Polish people.

*   *   *

Another thing I liked about the mass I went to with Mary was the music. There was a choir with all young people, accompanied by a piano and guitars. Even the conductor was young and good looking. I wish I could belong to that choir. But I'd probably have to be a member of the Catholic church. Maybe there's another choir in Mapleville that I could join. In a choir you don't have to be ravishingly beautiful or amazingly talented.

*   *   *

Tomorrow is Hallowe'en. Mary says there is nothing

like our North American October 31 in Poland. In Poland, November 1 is All Saints' Day. This is a very holy, serious day when everybody goes to the cemetery to honour the dead.

* * *

I showed Mr. Dunlop the stories I have so far from Mary. He said I should find some other people to interview also, because I need a "wider perspective". Mom gave me the name of a Polish Jewish woman at the college who would be "happy" to be interviewed by me. I was jolted by something this woman said. I hadn't realized that a lot of Polish people were and are anti-Semitic. I think my mother idealizes Poland when she talks to me about it.

* * *

What a Polish Jewish woman said when she was interviewed by Naomi at the college where she teaches English:

I am the daughter of Holocaust survivors from Krakow, Poland. During and after the war, my mother disguised herself as a Christian. After the war, she left Krakow and went to Wroclaw. She had become convinced that her sister had died in a Krakow hospital because anti-Semitic Polish doctors would not give her medicine. My mother had been settled in an apartment in Wroclaw for a several months when a Polish

Catholic priest dropped in and remarked that there were no Christian symbols on the walls.

My mother left Poland altogether that night, and she never returned.

I guess there has always been a love-hate relationship between Polish Jews and Polish Christians. Anyway, that's how I came to be born in West Germany.

When I was a child here in Canada, I got stories of bloated bodies piling up and of all the other horrors. I got these stories with my mother's milk. And it was not only the Nazis my mother told me about, it was also the Polish Catholics. The Polish Catholics were anti-semitic too.

By the time I was a teenager, I was pretty sick of these stories.

I was different from my mother, I decided. I yearned to be like the blonde English Canadian cheerleaders in my school. They were so pretty and peppy. When a Polish Catholic girl in my class asked if I spoke any Polish, I pretended I didn't.

Then I started to go out with this English Canadian boy. I thought he was incredibly handsome and nice. But one day he invited me to his house. There were Christian symbols on the walls: a cross and a picture of the Last Supper.

Suddenly, I felt very uncomfortable, and I broke up with the boy soon afterwards. I met my present husband when I was in college. He is also the son of Polish Jews.

Our marriage has been very happy.

We don't practice our religion. Yet we sent

our children to a Jewish school. There happened to be a Jewish school right across the road from where we lived in Toronto, so it was convenient.

Actually, my teenage daughter is going out with a boy who practises Wicca. It's some kind of old Celtic religion, I think. He's a nice boy. We're going to celebrate Hanukkah this year, just to show him what it's like.

Curtis

School is crap.
Work is crap.
Life is crap.
Diaries are crap.
My portfolio is crap.
I am crap.

Mary

The Little White Rose

One night when we come up from the shelter, our big strong house is just rubble and fire. We are poor now. We are refugees in our own country. Where before we owned a whole house, now we share one room with our neighbours.

After four years of war, many buildings have been destroyed. In the middle of a city, maybe one apartment building is left. In a whole apartment building, maybe one room is left.

Many people do not have a home. Neighbours

sleep beside each other. They sleep in rows, like fish in a can.

Many do not have food. Grandpa says there are Polish soldiers in German camps who have to eat their belts. Many do not have clean water. There is much sickness: cholera, typhus and tuberculosis. Most people do not have proper clothes. People cut up rubber tires to make shoes. They wear thin rags. They wear the same shirt day after day.

By the end of the war, people are exhausted, starving and sick. There is nothing. Nothing. We are all refugees in our own country.

After the war, a lady invites us to stay with her in her house for free. All during the war this lady vowed that, if her house were spared, she would share it with anyone who needed a roof over his head.

Her house is not strong. It is only made of wood. Other houses are made of brick. Still, when the bombs fall and the fires rage, only this lady's house is left standing. There is even one little white rose blooming in her garden. It is very beautiful. It smells sweet.

When this lady sees how I cry because my Daddy is not coming home, she gives the rose to me.

Anyway, after the war, we stay in this lady's house for a long time.

The lady's husband is dead. He was in the army like Daddy. The lady herself has a broken arm. She also has a little boy who is sad all the time, even though he is only five. Also, she has no food. So we help her.

Grandpa and Johnny fix things around this lady's house. Grandpa also goes and works for a butcher who pays him with soup bones.

Mommy sets the lady's arm. Mommy and Elizabeth also clean the house every day and cook. Elizabeth sits with the little boy quietly.

Johnny and I play with the little boy. We take him for walks. We make him laugh.

At first there are no seeds or animals. But eventually, Grandpa buys some seed potatoes, some chickens and a cow.

Grandpa is an old man now, but he is starting all over again. So is Mommy. So is Elizabeth. So are Johnny and I.

We three children start to go to school. There are no notebooks for school, no books, no pens, and no ink. And at the school there are no desks or chairs. We sit cross-legged on the floor. We write with pencil in the blank spaces of used notebooks.

We write our lessons, learn them, then rub them out.

We write over and over again in the same space, until the paper wears out.

And so it goes after the war.

In Canada and the United States, people watch killing on television and in movies, and they think it is nothing. Just fun. But they wouldn't think killing is nothing if they had lived with bullets and bombs aimed at *them*.

People don't recover so fast from war. No, they're never the same again.

Many years after the war, I am a grown woman, a doctor with a busy medical practice and children of my own. Suddenly one night I begin screaming in my sleep.

My little daughter, Anne, comes running into my room.

"Mommy, Mommy, what's wrong?" she asks.

"I was dreaming I was going to be killed," I explain, holding her close. "It was a nightmare. It's from the war long ago. Everything's all right now. You go back to sleep." Many years after the war, when he is a grown man, a construction engineer with a very responsible job, my brother travels back to where our old house once stood.

There is nothing. Not a brick. Not a fence post. Not a tree.

My big strong brother sits on a stump and cries.

Eva

What do I know about Hanna's childhood and youth? Very little, because she rarely talked about herself.

During the war, she was only a baby and toddler. She was only four years old when she was shipped with her mother and grandmother to Auschwitz after the Warsaw Uprising of 1944.

Hanna was born in Warsaw in late November, 1939. She was born in a room where the windows had been blown out by a bomb.

When Hanna was still a baby, a Nazi soldier tore Hanna from her mother's arms, threw her on the ground and hit her on the head with his gun butt.

Hanna's mother hid with her from the Nazis all one night in a cemetery.

Her mother was running along a Warsaw street one day. A Nazi bullet barely missed her, hit a wall, and bounced to the ground. Her mother scooped up the hot, squashed bullet and continued running.

Hanna kept the squashed bullet in a box in the kitchen. One day when I was visiting in 1979, Hanna showed me the bullet.

Hanna once described to me how everybody had to evacuate an apartment building while Nazi soldiers searched for Jews. The soldiers were convinced someone was hiding Jews.

Hanna remembered that when she, her mother, and her grandmother were shipped to Auschwitz, they were herded into a crowded box car. The box car had no roof. Hanna remembered looking at the stars and listening to her mother singing.

Hanna told me how the three escaped from the train before it reached Auschwitz.

The guards let the three off the train to seek medical attention at a clinic at a station. The doctors and nurses pushed them out the back door of the clinic and told them to run. Luckily the grandmother knew the town. Relatives in the town hid them.

* * *

The following poem was written by a Fulbright Scholar who spent a year in the 1970s teaching English at the University of Warsaw. Hanna met this scholar, David Reed, several times in Warsaw. When he returned to the United States, Reed published a slim collection of poetry about Poland I found a signed copy of Reed's collection in one of Hanna's boxes.

I See a Wounded Country

I see a wounded country
crawling through cubed multifoliate forms in triplicate
bleeding

    there's a movie crew underneath the bridge:
    the jews with their armbands and cardboard suitcases
    lined up to board the truck; the hurrying passers-by;
    the sleepy old peasant man with the big wooden wagon;
    the man with the attaché case and shiny boots and
    upturned collar; the ss-man with the dog; the man in
    the natty grey plus-fours riding by on a tandem bicycle:
    they've got to run through the scene again and again

rolling over
like the prince on the battlefield in Tolstoy's *War and Peace*
when the blue sky zoomed upwards

    there's a pigeon on the sidewalk that doesn't want
    to move: some man waiting for a bus tried to pick it
    up, a thin professional-looking lady said it's probably
    better to leave it, a child asked his mother if the
    birdy was lost, no dear she said its wing is broken,
    it was hit by a passing bus, the man who'd tried to pick
    it up said that's no. 155 I've got to go but I'd like
    to know what happens in the end: they'll run through
    the scene again and again

a beating heart
searching for
a body

Joe

I shovelled a foot of snow at my place and Eva's. Eva repaid by providing a week's worth of warm-in-the-microwave frozen meals on top of her usual great Saturday dinner.

A girl in one of my classes has been an exceptionally bad discipline problem. Utterly neurotic. Talks constantly to other students in class, talks back to me, heaps verbal abuse on everybody and everything, refuses to do her assignments.

I took her outside into the hallway alone. I told her she needed professional help. I gave her an ultimatum: "Don't come back to class until you have signed up for counselling!" The girl started shouting about my being "abusive". She claimed she was going to report me for "harrassment". Then she ran off.

Eva told me not to worry about what the student will say.

"After all," Eva said, "you've never stepped out of line with a student in twenty years, so the authorities are going to believe you, not her—even if she claims sexual harrassment. You were just doing your job. You were keeping order in the class while showing concern for an individual student."

In comparison to this student, Naomi is a delight. Naomi actually cracks pained smiles at my lousy jokes! In fact, Naomi is a well-balanced girl. She has begun blooming academically, and she seems to be outgrowing her self-centredness.

Naomi is quite upset about her friend, Dr. Kowalska, being cut back to part-time.

Week Nine

Naomi

Sunday, November 7, 1999

The trouble with Mary is that she is proud and stubborn. She is working harder than ever, so she will be able to do everything that the director told her to do. The director listed her duties on paper, "so there will be no disputes." Mary wants to prove that she is right and the director is wrong. Even if she wears herself out doing so.

"In Poland, in communism, woman cleaner never treated like this," said Mary.

"Some things in communism are probably better than some things in capitalism," I said.

"You are right," said Mary.

"You should get a lawyer and take the director to court," I said to Mary.

"I can't afford lawyer," Mary said.

After Mary and I finished work at the Rec Plex today, Mary came for dinner at our house, even though she was really tired. At our house, she didn't talk about work.

Joe gave me an interesting article from the *Mapleville Examiner* of October 9, 1999. The article, by Erica Church, reviews a film about a unique organization during World War II. Joe is going to order the film. He might use it in a class he teaches on ethics. Here is the article:

Extraordinary Heroism

"Kill Poles without mercy...all men, women and children of Polish descent and language... destroy all Poles." So ordered Hitler. Yet in Nazi-occupied Poland, some Poles did not think just about saving themselves. Although it was illegal to aid Jews and such aid was punishable by death, these Poles tried to save Jewish lives.

"*Zegota* is the story of extraordinary heroism... tantamount to *Schindler's List* multiplied a hundred-fold," wrote Zbigniew Brzezinski, former U.S. National Security Advisor, now a professor of American Foreign Policy at Johns Hopkins University.

Zegota is also a powerful new documentary film, directed by American Sy Rotter. The film is based on a 1994 book by Christian-Canadian Irene Tomaszewski and Jewish-Canadian Tecia Webowski. The 28-minute film combines riveting archival footage with fascinating contemporary interviews.

Zegota was a code word for Council for Aid to Jews in Occupied Poland. Established in 1942, the year the Nazis began to transport Jews in large numbers to death camps, Zegota saved about five thousand Jews before the war ended in 1945.

One of Zegota's most important contributions was providing "Aryan" documents for the Jews under its care. Zegota forged false baptismal, marriage, and death certificates, as well as identity and employment cards. This was done to help Jews pass as Christians.

Zegota manufactured about 50,000 documents. But three million Jews still lost their lives in wartime Poland.

"The help we provided was a small drop in an ocean of need," says Zegota activist Wladislaw Bartoszewski, an historian and a former Foreign Minister of Poland. "Only one or two per cent received help....I would warn Christians against smugness and self satisfaction."

"Too little was done," says another Zegota activist, Irena Sendlerowa, crippled and nearly killed by the Nazis for helping Jewish children. "Many Poles wanted to help. They wanted to, but they were afraid to."

Zegota was a "rare phenomenon" in Europe during World War II, according to Professor Yisrael Gutman, director of Yad Vashem's research center and former member of a Jewish fighting organization in the Warsaw ghetto. Yad Vashem, the "Holocaust Martyrs' and Heroes' Remembrance Authority", is located in Israel. It was established in 1953 to document the history of the Jewish people during the Holocaust.

"In Poland the effort to save Jews was much more dangerous than in other occupied countries," says Professor Gutman. "It is a kind of glory for the Polish people, even it is only the achievement of a very small minority. It was an expression of a great human spirit."

Zegota was "very important, morally important," according to Professor Alexander Gieysztor, President of Poland's Academy of Sciences and a former Home Army liaison with Zegota. "It was a kind of civic duty to help."

Members of Zegota came from differing backgrounds. They were mainly Catholic but also atheist, agnostic and Jewish.

This moving, thought-provoking film was produced by the Documentaries International Film & Video Foundation of Washington, D.C. for classroom and community screening.

* * *

I am angry with Sarah. She forgot about my audition for her band when I was too shy to mention it again.

I saw Curtis again in the hall at school. I marched up to him and asked him why he hadn't phoned the aquatic director at the Rec Plex about the job I got him.

"You could have told me that you were *not* interested," I said. "Why didn't you? I told the aquatic director that you *were* interested, and that you'd *phone* her."

"Look, Naomi, I'm really sorry about how rude I've been," Curtis said, getting red in the face. "I can't explain now because I have another class, but I can meet you at the front doors of the school in an hour."

"Okay," I said. "But don't be late. I won't wait."

What Curtis said when I met him later was both embarrassing and astounding. He said that he preferred to get his own jobs. He also said that he had been so impressed by me on the plane, he was too shy to phone me afterward.

"You were so well dressed, sophisticated and sure of yourself!" he said. "I didn't think you'd be interested in what I'm really like. You seemed like a privileged person who can't imagine why everyone else isn't as sociable as she is."

I told him that I had given him the wrong impression. I said that if he wants to see how weird my life is, he should come over to my house on Saturday evening and meet my family. He said he'd really like to come. I hope he'll keep his word this time.

Curtis

Lone Wolf saw She Wolf.

She Wolf saw Lone Wolf.

She Wolf attacked Lone Wolf. She bit and clawed.

Lone Wolf defended himself.

She Wolf wants Lone Wolf to visit her den and pack.

Q: Will lonely Lone Wolf win the paw of lovely She Wolf?

A: Wait for the first edition of our new cartoon strip entitled, "Something."

I got zero on the physics assignment. Mr. Bell noticed that Tom's and my answers were identical. I told him I'd work hard from now on.

"See that you do," he said ominously.

I felt humilitated.

I wish I could talk to Dad more often. He's in California now on business.

"Big bucks in the land of Bill Gates," he said. "I should have no problem buying you a car for Christmas. Maybe even a new one."

That was Dad's message in our epic, one-minute discussion today.

Mary

Who Is Mary?

Many students in my class have a special talent. Alice is a poet. The teacher always reads aloud what Alice writes. The class must discuss Alice's poem.

Frederick is a mathematician. No matter what question the teacher gives him, he can do the calculations—one, two, three and presto!

Peter is an artist. He draws pictures of everybody in the class—even the teacher. And his portraits really look like the person.

Beatrice is an actor. She is not plain like me. She is downright homely. But our school puts on a play, and Beatrice acts the part of a witch. Everybody says Beatrice is as good as a great actor in Warsaw. Now everybody knows that some day Beatrice will be famous.

As for me, I am good at many things. When the teacher asks us to write about the meaning of life, I write about what happened to my family in the war. The teacher reads aloud my composition. The class has to discuss it.

Sometimes the teacher asks me to go to the blackboard at the front of the class and show how I get the answer to a maths question, and often I am right.

I can draw the leaves of a plant accurately. Everybody can tell what kind of plant it is.

I am good at gymnastics, and I practice every day after school. Maybe I will win the national competition.

But I am not as good at sports as Johnny is. And I can't do my homework as fast as he can. Johnny finishes his lessons in one hour. Then maybe he fixes something for Mommy or Grandpa. Then he goes outside to play soccer with his friends. And he still gets the highest marks in his class!

I have to stay inside and study. Maybe I go out to the garden for a while and pull weeds, or else I help Grandpa with the animals, but then I have to come back inside and study some more. Meanwhile, Johnny is having fun.

Elizabeth doesn't care about getting good marks. She only studies a little bit. Then she cleans the house. Then she goes outside and walks with her gentleman friend. Still, Mommy says that Elizabeth is an angel.

I don't have a gentleman friend, and I am not an angel.

One day Elizabeth asks me to mail a letter to her gentleman friend. I go to the gymnastics club after school, and the gym club is near the post office.

Elizabeth has had a disagreement with her gentleman friend. She got angry and sent him away. Now she wants to apologize to him for sending him away.

I am in such a hurry that I forget to mail the letter.

So the next day Elizabeth doesn't get a letter back from her gentleman friend, and he doesn't come to call.

She asks me if I mailed the letter, and I say, "No, but I'll mail it tomorrow for sure."

But the next day I am in such a hurry that I forget to mail the letter again.

So again Elizabeth doesn't get a letter back from her gentleman friend, and he doesn't come to call. And again she asks me if I mailed the letter, and I say, "No, but I'll mail it tomorrow for sure."

Elizabeth still has long golden curls, but Mommy says she's like a nun, because she is so patient and loving and good.

I am not a nun. The third day I also forget to mail my sister's letter.

When she asks me if I mailed it, I say, "Yes, of course."

"Thank you," says Elizabeth, ever so sweetly. "You're a dear sister."

I say nothing and go and do my homework.

The next day when I come home from gym club, Elizabeth is crying because her gentleman friend didn't write her a letter, even though she wrote to *him*. And he didn't come to call.

I don't say anything, but I get on my bicycle and ride all the way to the post office without stopping, and I finally mail that letter.

Am I ever tired that evening as I do my homework! But I am happy, because I know that tomorrow Elizabeth will be smiling.

And she is!

After I win the national gymnastics competition, I

get very sick. I turn all yellow. The doctor diagnoses hepatitis and says my liver is diseased.

I was supposed to go to the Olympics, but after that sickness I can never do competitive sports again. I still like walking, though, and riding my bicycle.

And after being in the hospital, I want to be a doctor again—just like I did when I was a little kid.

Eva

Hanna's memories begin mostly after the war. One day when she was playing with some other children, these children began saying something derogatory about Jews. And she joined in. But then she saw the horrified look on her mother's face! She never joined in again.

Hanna and her mother lived for a long time after the war in a little log cabin in the Carpathians. The cabin had been built by an aunt who was a teacher in the village school. Hanna and her mother both had tuberculosis, so the mountain air was good for them.

Hanna attended the village school, fetched wood for the stove and helped in the garden.

When Hanna was a teenager, a priest named Karol Wojtyla used to come to the village from Krakow to lead young people on hiking trips in the mountains. This was the same Karol Wojtyla who became Pope John Paul II!

Father Wojtyla discussed religion during these hikes. Sometimes, he and his hikers would drop in to a little wooden church to pray.

Everyone would be wearing hiking clothes while

they prayed. Even Father Wojtyla. And everyone had to address Father Wojtyla as "Uncle", rather than "Father". If the communist authorities knew he was a priest, he and his young hikers would be in trouble.

When I met her in 1979, Hanna still liked hiking in forests and high places. She also liked discussing philosophy, art and literature.

Hanna and her mother obtained an apartment in Warsaw by winning a lottery.

She and her mother received occasional packages of food and clothing from relatives living abroad. They also received help from another priest whom Hanna called "Uncle".

When I visited Hanna in Warsaw, "Uncle" still dropped by from time to time with a bouquet of flowers and some meat and vegetables from his country parish.

"Uncle" never stayed long. Just long enough for tea and a chat, and then he was gone.

Hanna spoke once only about her "ten lost years". These were the years following her mother's suicide.

Yet she acquired a Master's degree in art history, and a Master's degree in library science. She began to work at the National Library in Warsaw.

She said she had to relearn everything. The relearning was slow and painful.

* * *

One of the poems in Reed's collection is dedicated to Hanna. This long poem, titled "Warsaw Reverie", is complex and prosey, but its refrain is brief and lyrical. The refrain was apparently inspired by a glimpse Reed caught of Hanna standing in a crowded, jerking tramway in Warsaw. Reed had already met Hanna several times at the National Library, where she worked. Here is the refrain:

She is tall and within her is some strength of mind,
and she sways. The wind is kissing her eyes and lashes,
and she sways. The wind is bringing the rain and ashes,
and she sways. Within her is some strength of mind.

Joe

The out-of-control student was hauled up by the head of her department. She was given a long and serious talking-to. When I phoned the head, she was completely supportive of me. Other teachers have been having the same kinds of problems with this student, or worse. Case closed. (Joe, old man, where was your self confidence?)

Back to the usual grind. Mid-terms this week. Enough committee work to choke a horse. Enough paperwork to...whatever.

Some good shots of the early snowfall.

Both boys are doing well in school. Their teachers were very positive during parents' night. Apparently the boys' school has the most problems of any in the city. The school brought in a Special Ed teacher full time last month for the rest of the semester.

"So many single-parent families," said Jerry's Grade Six teacher, who surely knows that Jill and I are divorced. I guess I'm a decent father after all.

Week Ten

Naomi

Sunday November 14, 1999

If it weren't for Mary, I'd quit this stupid job right away. Mary needs my moral support, and my physical help.

Mary says many people think cleaners are "nothing." I say many people regard a cleaner as a machine. A machine is not human.

You finish cleaning a window. The next minute, a parent lets her kid smear the window with his sticky hands. You keep cutting your hand on the towel rack when you put the new rolls in. And the director is sure it's your fault, not the cheap design. You carefully put the mop away clean. But then some higher-up staff member, like the accountant or the social director, borrows it to clean up a spill. This well-paid, full-time person does not bother rinsing out the mop. So it is dirty when you have to use it again. Then the customers plug the toilets with sanitary pads, even though the sign says not to. So the cleaner fetches the plunger and plunges this disgusting stuff, until the toilet stops flooding over. Plunging toilets is the janitor's job. But the janitor is busy with something else. So, to be helpful, the cleaner does it instead. Now the cleaner works extra time to finish her written-down cleaning quota, even though she is not paid for this time.

I am very worried about Mary. Often, towards the end of our shift, her lips get blue, and she gets chest pains. She says these symptoms are caused by the chemicals we use to clean windows and mirrors.

"I tell director we must not use so many chemicals, but he no listen me," Mary says.

"Tell him how your lips get blue and you get chest pains," I say.

"What for?" she says. "I already told him. He no listen to no old womans."

"You should see a doctor about your symptoms," I say.

"What for?" she snaps. "I *am* doctor."

"Doctors aren't supposed to treat themselves, or their family and friends," I say. "That's what Sarah says. Her father is a doctor."

"I have no time," she says. "I am starting from zero. When can I go to doctor?"

Mary tries to appear confident, but I think that she is worried about her health too. She is alone here in Canada, and our system seems cruel.

* * *

Sarah and I are becoming true friends. I told her I was angry at her for making me fail that biology test, and for forgetting my audition for her band. After I did this, we had a so-called "heart-to-heart" talk, and Sarah apologized for being inconsiderate. She also said that her family is falling apart.

Sarah's father moved in with his secretary. Her brother moved in with a drug-pusher friend. Her mother cries all the time and blames her father for committing adultery and leading his son astray. Her mother also tells Sarah that Sarah is her "last hope". Sarah thinks she (Sarah) is going to crack up if she doesn't move out too. She's not planning to go to Paris or New York now. She wants to move in with her boyfriend. Her boyfriend rents a house with three other guys here in Mapleville.

* * *

Curtis came over to our house for dinner last Saturday. He got along well with my mother, Joe and me. At first, Curtis mostly listened to everybody, but gradually he began to relax and talk.

At the dinner table, Curtis seemed interested when Joe talked about growing up without a father. Joe's father died when Joe was eight. Joe only had an uncle who was too busy with his business to pay much attention to him. That's why Joe is very careful to spend as much "quality time" as possible with his sons. Curtis nodded and looked sympathetic when Joe said all this.

Curtis seemed impressed when Mom told him that Hanna had devoted a lot of her time in her last years to caring for several young men with AIDS. He seemed even more impressed when Mom told him that Hanna had been an art historian. He was grateful when Mom said she had lots of art books that Hanna had given her over the years, and that Curtis could borrow them. Curtis said there aren't many good art books at the Mapleville Library, and he has already memorized them.

After dinner, Joe and Mom went over to Joe's place to watch some intellectual videos. Mary visited with Hanna, and Curtis and I went to see *Tarzan*. After the movie, Curtis and I went for sundaes, and then for a walk. We talked for hours. He told me how the animators made *Tarzan*. I told him about how worried I was about Mary. He said that, unfortunately, there are no cleaning jobs available at the grocery store where he works.

Curtis talked more than he had on the plane. He even laughed. Curtis wants to be a visual artist. He would rather draw pictures than study academic subjects: that's why he failed Grade Twelve last year. Curtis is mostly a serious person, but he also appreciates humour, especially cartoons. Like me, Curtis has some problems at home. His father left him and his mother about two years ago. His father fell in love with another man, "came out", and went to start a new life in Edmonton, but that didn't work out. Curtis loves his father a lot. He respects him as a brilliant guy who tries hard to be a great father. But Curtis finds it hard to forgive his father for leaving, and for not having much time for him right now. Curtis says he hates his mother's friend, Steve, who is an ignorant bully. Curtis says he doesn't usually tell people about his father being gay.

"Even though I'm not gay myself," Curtis said, "I worry that if people know about Dad's orientation, they'll label *me* and make my life a lot more difficult than it already is. I just wish Dad had stuck around, so I could still do father-son stuff with him. We talk about everything—computers, birds, whatever. All Steve talks about is organized sports. He thinks every 'normal' guy adores sports on TV. Personally, I like getting exercise, but I hate organized sports. Especially team sports. I'd rather bike, hike or canoe outdoors by myself."

This was the best Saturday evening of my entire life. I *knew* Curtis was the right guy for me. My horoscope for Saturday said that I am "an attractive, warm-hearted person who is good with people." I hope Curtis agrees.

Curtis

Had a good time at Naomi's house.

Mary is difficult to understand, because her English is so bad. But she is nice.

So is Hanna, who said only one sentence to me. She is too sick to talk much.

Eva is a great cook and generous. She said I could borrow her art books any time.

Joe is a great guy. Hulking grizzly bear, but as gentle as a white-tailed deer.

Naomi is bee-yoo-tee-full!

Somewhere deep in the boreal forest, He Wolf howls.

"She Wolf," he howls, "I woof you!"

Woo-oo-oo-oof!

Mary

Let Us Out

I am sure I want to be a doctor. But sometimes I am not sure of myself. Am I good enough? Will my marks be high enough? Mommy and Grandpa can't afford to send me to medical school. I have to win a scholarship. I do!

Then I am in medical school, and all we students have to work very hard. There are long hours in the classroom, long hours in the laboratory, long hours in the hospital, and long hours studying in our rooms. It is difficult to find time to eat and sleep, but I do. It is difficult to find time to have fun, but I do.

Mommy sends Johnny and me back to university with food parcels. Johnny is in engineering school in the same city as my medical school. We take care of each other.

I tell him that his girlfriend is seeing another man. I sew the buttons back on his shirts. He takes me to dances with his friends. He makes sure his friends are nice to me.

I don't have too much money, so I make my own dresses and do my own hair. I wear the same dress to a few parties, then I sell it to get money to make another dress. Also, I make dresses for the other girls.

I am sewing as I read a medical text. Read, stitch, stitch, stitch. Read, stitch, stitch, stitch. Read, stitch, stitch, stitch.

When we finish our medical exams, we want to celebrate. The other students say to me, "Mary, you don't drink, so you must guard the door. You must see that we do not go outside, shout on the streets and get into trouble."

At this time in Poland, it was very dangerous to express your opinions of the communist regime publicly. No sooner had one war ended in Poland, than another had begun. As the Nazis fled, the Soviets invaded. After World War II, the Cold War. Now war was not about killing the body—unless we openly resisted. It was about killing freedom.

We medical students have to pass an exam about communism. About politics! I hate politics! This is ridiculous. Politics have nothing to do with medicine.

If we don't pretend to believe in communism, we must leave medical school. One student even goes to jail for mocking the system. One professor is sent to Siberia.

You know what it's like to be sent to Siberia? People are crowded worse than cattle in a box car of a long train. Everybody has to pee and poop in a pot in the middle of the box-car floor. There's no toilet paper. There's no privacy.

You have no change of clothes. You have no place to wash. You are dirty and stinking. Everybody is dirty and stinking.

Then, when you get to Siberia, there's not enough food. Just watery porridge, if you're lucky. In summer, there's hard labour on farms. In winter, there's severe cold—months and months in the deep freeze. And you don't have proper clothes to keep warm.

Often, of course, you die.

Stalin, who is the ruler now, is as bad as Hitler. Millions of people in his own country starve to suit his whims. Millions suffer.

Anyway, at our graduation party, the other students drink vodka, dance, sing and get louder and louder in expressing their true opinions about politics. I don't drink. I never do. I lock the door of the house where we are partying, and I hide the key.

The other students are becoming aggressive. They are determined to go outside into the streets. They want to wake up the whole city by singing and shouting.

"Let us out!" they shout. "We want freedom *now!*"

They crowd around me and bully me.

"Give us the key, Mary," they say. "We want the key *now!*"

"Just a moment," I say. "I can't find the key. I don't remember where I left it. I'm looking for it. You go lie down and rest, while I look for it."

Finally, I get all the girls lined up and resting on one bed. And I get all the boys lined up and resting on the other bed. And they all sleep safe and sound until morning.

Instead of going to jail, they all go off to different hospitals in different cities and towns all over Poland.

We begin our work as doctors.

Eva

Naomi seems to have "adopted" this boy Curtis, as well as Doctor Kowalska. Curtis is a nice boy, but I wish Naomi weren't so sudden and passionate in her likes and dislikes. I suppose she'll outgrow this wild intensity.

You can be "adopted" at any age, according to Hanna. Hanna adopted me in 1979, when I was a bit older than Naomi is now. She adopted me emotionally, not legally.

When Hanna adopted me, I was an emotional orphan.

133

My father had ignored me, my mother had never wanted me, and Grandmother Goralski had been severe and narrow-minded. I thought I had no feelings at all.

Actually, I had feelings of guilt, anger and despair. Only at that time, I didn't know I had those feelings. During Hanna's first few years in Canada, she stayed with my grandmother and me in Edmonton. One day Hanna and I learned that our father had died suddenly, before either of us had met him. (We had been intending to visit him in Colorado, where he lived. We were waiting until my Grandmother Goralski did not need constant care.) Typically, Hanna was more concerned with my feelings than with her own.

Several times I cried on and on, while Hanna sat beside me silently.

Then I talked, while Hanna listened, commenting rarely and briefly. I said that I was angry at my parents for abandoning me. She said that my anger was understandable.

I insisted that Hanna would abandon me too. She promised she would stay with me, as long as I needed her.

She also said that, when she was my age, she herself felt angry at the world. She was angry because her mother was alone, except for Hanna, and burdened by enormous problems.

To discover what emotions Hanna felt in the present, I had to be very observant, because normally her face was an impassive mask. One day, she and I were strolling through an exhibition at an art gallery. Suddenly we came upon a picture of a coffin. On Hanna's face I noticed a flash of surprised recognition. *This* is meaningful! Had I not been watching her closely, I would have missed a valuable clue. The expression disappeared as quickly as it had appeared.

The clue indicated that Hanna was still affected by her mother's suicide. Hanna was in her final year of university when her mother killed herself. Hanna came home after an absence of a few hours, and she found her mother dead.

Hanna did explain to me why her mother had ended her life, but never *how*. Her mother had been exhausted from her own illness, tuberculosis, and from the illnesses of other family members whom she was nursing. Also, she had been depressed. A psychiatrist had told Hanna that this depression was a result of the terrible experiences her mother had endured during the Second World War in Poland.

Although Hanna could explain her mother's suicide, ultimately she could not overcome its devastating effect on her psyche. Once Hanna told me that I had "freed" her. I think she meant by this that I had freed her from the bonds of guilt she felt about her mother. She still identified with her mother, however, and finally wanted to demonstrate that her mother had not been wrong to despair. Her mother was not *wrong*, she was *ill*.

So was Hanna in these last years. Yet she was also far-seeing and heroic.

Joe

Naomi brought an interesting young man home for supper. The kid could use more self-confidence, but he's got a strong, original character. He is artistic,

135

humorous and bright. But not keen on school. He seems to think I'm half decent—for an old guy.

There's hope! (No fool like an old fool?)

The grind continues. I think one reason I'm losing interest is because the level of psychology and sociology taught at the college is relatively elementary. Eva's technology courses seem more sophisticated. Or do I think this because I am ignorant about hard science?

I asked Eva to live with me, even marry me. I said in one household we could help each other more than we do now.

Of course, Eva said: "Wait!"

Hanna is failing rapidly. I was selfish to pressure Eva now. What's the hurry? Is the frantic "Y2K" hype getting to me?

Making conversation with Naomi's admirer, Curtis, I told him about getting a lesson on predicting weather when I was a boy in elementary school. All the other children looked at the barometer and predicted sunshine and fair weather. Only I predicted rain. And I was right! Why? Because the next day was Wednesday. My Mom always did her laundry on Wednesday, and she hung it out to dry.

Curtis actually laughed aloud at my silly story. Naomi was shocked!

Of course when I told the story to my own boys, they said: "Da-ad! That is so du-umb!"

Week Eleven

Naomi

Saturday, November 20, 1999

Today as Mary and I were finishing our shift, her chest pains got very bad, and suddenly she told me calmly, "Call emergency!"

I ran to the red telephone on the wall beside the swimming pool and lifted the receiver. That automatically calls an ambulance. The paramedics came in four minutes, put Mary on a stretcher and took her to the emergency department of the Mapleville hospital. I went with her. She didn't have to wait. She was put on a bed right away. She was constantly monitored by the nurses and doctors.

I called Mom from the hospital to tell her I wouldn't be home for dinner. Mom came to the hospital right away. She sat with me in the emergency waiting room. "Joe will stay with Hanna and give her some dinner," she said.

"That's nice of him," I said.

"He is nice, darling, and I hope some day you'll see

that," said Mom. "But I remember how I hated my stepfather George, so I don't want to force anything on you."

"You're not forcing anything on me," I said. Then I started crying. "Everybody seems to be dying. Aunt Hanna, and now Mary."

"Doctor Kowalska is in good physical condition," said Mom. "And she's not very old. She'll survive."

At about eight o'clock this evening, a nurse came and said that Mary has to stay in intensive care overnight and maybe for a few days. So Mary might not survive.

Sorry this is so short, Mrs. Henderson. I'm sure you will understand. I will now fill up more pages by printing out some interviews and other objective information from my history project and sticking them here in my journal.

* * *

What *The Breakup of the Soviet Union* by B. Harbor said about the Hungarian Revolution: "23 October 1956. Soviet tanks sent in to aid Hungarian communist government in dealing with demonstrations. Soviet troops leave, but return on 4 November when new Hungarian government declares neutrality. Hungarians rebel against Soviet army, but Soviets overwhelm resistance. 30,000 Hungarians die in uprising."

* * *

What a Hungarian said when interviewed by Naomi at her high school where he teaches music:

I was born in Budapest, Hungary, in 1948. Of course, Hungary was one of the "satellite" countries behind the so-called "Iron Curtain". I wasn't very old when I learned what Stalinism meant. We were Jewish, although we didn't actually practice our religion. One Saturday when I was in kindergarten, my father took me to see a synagogue.

We didn't go inside. We just looked at the outside. But I was pretty excited about this experience, so I told my kindergarten teacher about it. The next day my father was picked up by the secret police and beaten severely.

Although my mother worked as a secretary for a member of the communist party, my father had always refused to become a communist. Anyway, another night in 1956, a black car with black windows took my father away. They beat him again. They kept him all night.

We left Hungary pretty soon after this. As our car drove through the streets of Budapest that night, I saw the bodies of revolutionaries hanging on telephone poles.

We boarded a train that took us near the Austrian border. When we got off the train, we ran for the border. Eventually, we got to Vienna. We stayed in a refugee camp.

Our plane landed at Gander, Newfoundland, on Christmas Eve, 1956. It was dark and, except for the runway, the airport tarmac was covered with deep snow. My father had to carry my little sister over to the terminal. We ate hotdogs and french fries with ketchup.

My mother started crying. She didn't stop crying for about two years. She always hated Canada.

My father did not hate Canada. He was grateful for the opportunities this country had offered him and his children. For example, my sister and I could go to university. When he was a young man in Hungary, no Jew was allowed to attend university.

*   *   *

What a Polish lifeguard said when Naomi interviewed him at the Recreation Centre:

I'm from Wroclaw. I have been here in Canada four years. It's good here because there are so many economic opportunities. Right now I have three jobs, plus I go to university. None of the jobs pays that good, but still I can get ahead pretty quick, and in a few years I'll have a high-paying job. I want to be maybe a high school teacher or an athletics coach. At the same time, I can help my mother back in Poland. She's on pension now, but she does not have enough to live on.

*   *   *

What a young Polish woman said when Naomi interviewed her at her delicatessan:

I have only been in Canada eight years, but

already I have my own shop. It's not much. I'm not getting rich. With my husband's salary, we just make enough to live on. We support our baby daughter and make our mortgage payments, and already we've sent enough money so my parents can come for a visit. My husband is Polish too. He has a construction job. We came at the same time. We were teenagers still. But already we were in love.

I took English lessons for a while, but I quit. I don't need perfect English to do what I'm doing. My customers understand me. I worked in a meat shop back home, so I know about selling Polish meats and sausages. When I first came here, I worked in someone else's shop, so I know Canadian business. Yeah, Canada is a good place. Our best friends now are some English Canadians. They are our neighbours. They are Newfoundlanders. I'm glad we came.

* * *

Grandma just phoned me from Edmonton and invited me to go to Hawaii for Christmas with her and George, all expenses paid! I said I'd phone her back next weekend and let her know. I explained that my best friend was seriously ill in the hospital. I didn't tell Grandma that Mary is older than she is. She might get jealous. I also didn't tell Grandma that I was working as a cleaner. She would not approve. I just said I was really busy.

Curtis

Mom got back with Steve today while I was at school. Also, she found my diary and read it out loud to Steve. She said that Steve did not appreciate how I had described him. She told me these interesting facts while she was making dinner, and I was helping her.

Luckily, she said this before Steve got back from fetching his stuff to move in with us again. Otherwise, I might have killed someone.

Instead, I told my mother: (1) She has no right to invade my privacy. (2) She is crazy to get back with Steve. (3) I'm leaving.

She started screaming at me that she absolutely had to read my diary to find out what was going on with me. She absolutely had to find this out, because I never tell her anything. Just like Dad never told her anything. She also screamed that I have absolutely no right to tell her what to do, or what not to do.

Before she screamed any more hysterical drivel, I left the house. I walked around for a couple of hours, and then I went to see Joe Dekkers. Joe had told me to drop in some time and see his photos and dark room.

Joe shook hands with me, invited me in and made us a couple of his and Eva's "famous Sloppy Joe sandwiches". We talked for a couple of hours.

In the end, we made a deal that I can live at Joe's house for a while. I can sleep on an old couch in his basement. I can also eat at his house. In return for my room and board, I will help Joe cook and clean up around his place, shovel all the snow at his and Eva's houses, babysit his boys on the weekends sometimes, and generally make myself useful.

I phoned my mother about ten o'clock that evening. I told her where I was, and what I was doing. I told her I needed my own space. She started screaming more drivel, so I hung up.

I went home the next day while Mom and Steve were out. I packed a duffle bag and garbage bag with my stuff, took them over to Joe's and officially moved in.

Joe started as a bouncer, then became a cop. He picked up a couple of university degrees, worked with young offenders, then started teaching. Now he wants to be "downwardly mobile". He wants to drive trucks and do photography.

I'm going to check out Joe's T'ai Chi class tomorrow.

Mary

Country Doctor

Elizabeth is a nurse. She is already married. She has a baby girl. Johnny is already an engineer, working on huge construction projects. Finally, I have my first job. I am a country doctor. I am far from the big-city hospital where I interned. I am also far from my brother, sister and mother. I am on my own.

I am a pretty good doctor, but sometimes I make mistakes. The first mistake is with a three-year-old girl. She is very sick. She has a high temperature. Her neck is as rigid as though she has swallowed a stick, and she is unconscious. I diagnose meningitis, but, at the city hospital where I send her, the more experienced doctor diagnoses severe bronchitis.

The second mistake is with a woman who has pain in

143

her lower back and whose urine is abnormal. I diagnose kidney trouble. But not long after I send her to the city hospital, her legs become paralyzed. She has polio.

The third mistake is with a man whose symptoms indicate typhus. Or so I think. When the doctors in the city hospital operate, they find that he has an ulcerated bowel.

Yes, I do make mistakes, but usually I diagnose correctly. The city doctors ask me how I can be right so often. Out in the country, I don't have sophisticated equipment and tests.

"I use my eyes and my fingers, and I listen carefully to my patient," I say. "I ask many questions. And I always tell the patient to return to me, if he is not feeling better in one or two days."

One patient comes back in two days.

He says: "Doctor, I am taking the medicine you gave me, but I don't feel any better."

I ask: "How often do you take the medicine?"

"One in the morning, one at noon, and one at night," he replies.

"But that is not enough!" I exclaim. "I prescribed four pills right away, then two every four hours, and all through the night too. You should have taken twenty pills by now, and you've only taken six."

I show the patient the directions I wrote on his bottle of pills. He goes home and does as he was told.

A farmer comes and asks me to cure his sheep. His sheep has a broken leg.

"I am not an animal doctor!" I protest. "I'm a people doctor!"

"Please help!" he pleads. "There is no one else."

"Oh, all right," I sigh. "But I make no promises."

I treat the sheep as though it is a human being: I put its leg in a cast. I have no idea whether the sheep's leg will get better, but it does. The leg heals perfectly.

Then another farmer comes and asks me to cure his cow.

"I am not an animal doctor!" I protest again. "I am a people doctor!"

But the farmer will not listen to my protests, and finally I go and help his cow. And for the rest of the years that I remain in the country, that farmer supplies me with fresh milk every morning—for free. The bottle of milk is on my doorstep when I open the door.

One day as I am doing my rounds, someone asks me to visit a very old woman who is very ill. The woman must be ninety years old. She has pneumonia. I give her medicine, and she gets better. Because she is very poor, I say, "Don't worry about my fee." But she shows up at my house a few weeks later with sorrel leaves she has picked by the roadside for making soup.

Because I know how far she has walked with those leaves, I begin to cry.

One day I am visiting the reform school. The reception room is filled with young offenders waiting for inoculations. Suddenly, someone runs into the room and tells me that a child at the school is so sick he may die at any moment. I grab my medical bag and start running too. I forget to lock the medicine cabinet that sits in one corner of the reception room.

One hour later, when I return to the reception room after treating the sick child, I remember about the medicine cabinet. I almost panic. I know these young offenders, who have been waiting all this time in the reception room, have committed all sorts of crimes. Surely, they discovered that the cabinet is unlocked! Surely, they stole some drugs!

But when I check the drugs in the cabinet that evening, I find nothing missing. The next day I tell the young offenders how well they behaved. That Christmas, I invite them to a party at my house.

Most country people are poor. Often, I do not allow my patients to give me money, for if they do, they will not be able to afford medicine. I tell them: "You must not pay for my services, but pray for my health." Many people must have prayed for my health, because for a long time I was very healthy.

As well as milk, sorrel and prayers, the country people give me a free house and free vegetables and fruit. I ask them to donate some food to the reform school, instead of to me. And they do.

Eva

When she first came to Canada, Hanna attended mass more often than she had in Poland. Later, she became alienated from the Catholic Church. She decided the church was "detached from social reality." Now, when she is dying, she refuses to see a priest.

She has asked only for communion wafers. When I went to the church to get the wafers, the priest said he had never received such a request, but he sent a full bag of wafers. She ate only one. I left the rest in the backyard for the squirrels.

Then one day Hanna asked to hear a recording she

gave me long ago: Penderecki's *Passion and Death of Our Lord Jesus Christ According to St. Luke.*

She spent hours listening to the long piece.

She made no comment.

Hanna knows as much about dying as she does about living, perhaps more. So many people died while she was growing up in Poland, during the war and after.

As she lies dying, she wants to be near her "close ones". She wants to be near them as they live their everyday lives. To her last breath, she wants to teach them.

Now, she is teaching me about dying. For so many years, she taught me about living. "Much sunshine," she would say during all those years, instead of saying "Goodbye."

"This capitalist society has a negative selection process," she would say. "Those who are successful in this society often lack the best human qualities."

"I have a certain attitude toward life," she would say.

"Don't exaggerate," she'd say.

"Don't be aggressive," she'd say.

"Look at life," she'd say.

She likes to be silent and still in her room. She likes to listen to the sounds of the family and friends of her adopted daughter.

All the ordinary, everyday sounds of people who love each other.

Joe

I've got a boarder: Naomi's friend, Curtis. He needs another, older fellow to talk to.

And I need another, younger fellow to talk to. I was getting tired of reading every evening. And writing my "lonely hearts" diary.

Curtis has had a difficult time for the past few years. It's a measure of his strength of character that he hasn't gotten into big trouble. He has, however, become wary of our so-called civilization. He says he feels like a wild animal in a cage.

Both Curtis's parents phoned me. Curtis's father seems like a decent fellow. He's trying to come back from a business failure, and to get his personal life together at the same time. Curtis's mother is okay too. Just narrow-minded, and overly worried about her son.

Curtis says his mother's boyfriend assaulted him. I told Curtis I thought his mother should have let him press charges. I also told him he should not have had to tolerate the man's verbal abuse.

My boys wanted to shop for ski equipment the other day. They were outraged when I dragged them to a second-hand store. Tough.

Got some good shots of cumulus clouds in Eva's backyard yesterday, while "babysitting" Hanna.

Naomi's doctor friend has had a heart attack and been hospitalized. It seems serious.

What next?

Sometimes I feel like Atlas holding up the pillars of the universe. Or is it Sisyphus rolling a boulder up a mountain?

Or am I turning into a boulder myself? An ancient mountain?

Week Twelve

Naomi

Sunday, November 28, 1999

Last Sunday morning at eight, when Mary and I were supposed to start work, I phoned the receptionist at the Rec Plex and told her what had happened to Mary the afternoon before. I also told her that I was quitting. I said that I would write a letter of resignation to the director and deliver it on Monday. I spent the rest of the morning talking to Mom and writing my letter.

In the afternoon I went to the hospital. Curtis came with me. Curtis thinks I was right to quit the Rec Plex job.

"You don't owe them anything," he said. "And besides, there are lots of other rotten, minimum-wage jobs out there."

Curtis is going to ask about a job for me as a cashier at the grocery store where he works.

They wouldn't let Curtis into Intensive Care, only me. I am listed as next-of-kin.

The nurse asked if I was Mary's granddaughter.

"You look so much alike," she said.

Visitors are not allowed to stay for long in Intensive Care. This is a medium-sized room with low lighting and quiet machines beside the beds. Mary was hooked up to several machines. She smiled and squeezed my hand. Now that she is in a Canadian hospital, she seems more trusting of our society.

I told Mary that I was relieved she was finally getting proper care for her chest pains. She told me that she was too. "Canadian nurses and doctors are very good," she said.

I told her that I would come back again in the evening with Mom.

* * *

Mom went with me to the hospital in the evening. Mary was out of Intensive Care. She was in a regular hospital room with three other women in the same room. Mom brought flowers for Mary and kissed her on the cheek. Then Mary, Mom and I had a discussion.

Mary has worse problems than we thought. The doctors found this out when they saw X-rays of her chest. Mary has breast cancer, as well as a heart condition! She has to have an operation to remove the cancer. But her heart is not healthy enough to endure an operation right away, so she has to rest at home for about two weeks.

Mary is worried that, even after two weeks' rest, her heart will not be healthy enough. She is afraid that she might die during the operation. But she still wants to have it. She agrees with the Canadian doctors that it's the right thing to do.

Mary *was* worried about money too, but she isn't any more.

Mom told Mary that she can receive unemployment insurance, a disability pension, or welfare. Then, after she has been a landed immigrant for ten years, she can receive the old age pension and a guaranteed income supplement. Mary was relieved to hear this. So was I.

Mom also told Mary: "There is no use your hiring a lawyer to protest your unfair treatment at the Recreation Complex. Law cases take not only much money, but also much time. Of course, the local newspaper could make a front-page story out of what happened to you. The director of the Rec Plex might get fired."

"I don't want make no trouble," said Mary. "Not for director, not for nobody. I never made no trouble for nobody in my whole life. I want forget about this bad experience. That's all. I not think about it more. It make me more sick to think about it."

Then Mom also told Mary that her daughter could come here to look after her. Mary said her daughter could not get out of Poland, but Mom said she could.

"It's an emergency," Mom said, "and your daughter is not trying to emigrate permanently. Besides, Joe and I will sponsor her. We are Canadian citizens and financially secure."

There are times when having an experienced, professional, engineer/teacher for a mother is handy. I was impressed by how Mom started solving Mary's problems efficiently. Even though Mom was (and is) under a lot of stress herself, she was calmly helpful to Mary.

As we were walking home from the hospital, Mom

said that, although Mary is a good friend, I must not panic and forget my school work. I said that, now that I have quit working at the Rec Plex, I will have plenty of time for school *and* helping Mary. I said I had "adopted" Mary. Mom said she was proud of me.

"When Mary gets out of the hospital, she can just rest," I said. "If I have to pay her landlady with my own money to cook meals for Mary, then I will. Or I'll take dinner to Mary after school—after I've heated up something for Hanna."

"Hanna's not eating much anyway," said Mom, sighing. "Many days she has little more than a glass of water. I'll try to get home earlier this week. I should be able to. The semester is winding down."

When we got home, Joe was still there, reading a book at the kitchen table. Joe promised to drive Mary home from the hospital when they let her out. He also offered to do the paperwork for getting Mary's daughter to Canada.

* * *

I phoned Grandma this evening to thank her for inviting me to go to Hawaii. I explained that I couldn't go with her and George this time because I am needed here. I promised that I would write her letters during the winter, and that I would visit her next summer. She said she would send me a postcard as soon as she got to Hawaii.

Sarah phoned me just after I finished talking with Grandma. I told her what had happened to Mary, and she was very sympathetic. Sarah told me that her father has moved back home. Actually his secretary, who is much younger, "dumped him." I told Sarah that she is lucky. Her father might be behaving immaturely, but at least he lives in the same house as her, so she can see what he's like.

* * *

Here is the letter of resignation that I wrote to the director of the Rec Plex:

> Dear Sir:
> I am resigning my part-time position as a cleaner at the Recreation Complex in order to protest what I feel is the very unfair treatment of two full-time female cleaners. These cleaners were made part-time employees after they had been full-time for several years. They lost their benefits and were paid less, even though they were expected to do the same amount of work. I definitely feel that this unfair situation was the main cause of one of these employees, Dr. Mary Kowalska, becoming seriously ill.
> Yours truly,
> Naomi Goralski

Curtis

Joe and I get along great. School and work are okay. Joe says Eva and Naomi need a lot of "emotional support" these days. They need us to listen to them.

Mom sent a cop around to check on Joe and me.

The cop said that, since I am over eighteen, there's nothing Mom can do if I don't want to stay with her any more. The cop was an old guy who knew Joe. He shook hands with Joe and me as he left.

Joe and I are busy. I've started taking judo lessons. When I went to check out Joe's T'ai Chi class, I watched some judo black belts working out in another room. I decided I preferred judo.

At the Christmas break, we're going to Toronto together to look for some equipment for Joe's photography in antique shops and second-hand stores. We're also going to visit some art galleries.

Joe says he was pretty lonely "batching" by himself. He says he used to have a drinking problem. He dried out with a good alcoholism counsellor, once he faced his problem. He never touches booze now.

Joe used to push people around, like Steve does. But he realized that kind of mindless aggression is useless. Also destructive.

I do the grocery shopping, because Joe hates doing that. He does the laundry, because I hate doing that.

Mary

Lost and Found

The last year I worked as a country doctor, my mother came to stay with me. After Grandpa died, she stayed one year with Elizabeth, one year with Johnny, and then one year with me. Sadly, I soon discovered that Mom was seriously ill. She was dying.

Soon she is so sick that she is in bed most of the time. When I am not at home, a neighbour comes in and gives my mother her meals. Unfortunately, I am not home most of the time, because my medical practice keeps me very busy.

After I return each night, I do what I can for my mother. I feel guilty that I can't do more, but she sees how tired I am. She says: "Don't worry. I am happy to lie quietly in your house. That is enough. The neighbour takes care of me quite well."

Still, I worry. Sometimes I wake up in the middle of the night. I slip into my mother's bedroom to listen to her breathing. I know that soon her breathing will stop.

One night she calls to me. I go into her bedroom. She folds me in her arms, and she holds me tight.

"My child!" she exclaims, and then she dies.

After my mother dies, living alone is difficult. I have made many friends in the country, but still I feel too sad.

My gentleman friend, Paul, lives in a big city. The city is several hours away by train. He comes every Sunday, but that is not enough. He wants me to marry him and move to his city. Finally, I decide he is right. It is time to start a family.

Our first child, Adam, is named after my father.

When Adam is two, I take him with me to the hospital where I work now. A woman is selling doughnuts just inside the door.

"Doughnut, please, Mommy!" says Adam.

"You sit right here," I say, lifting the chubby little child onto a bench. "And don't move!"

I turn my back for a moment to buy the doughnut, and Adam disappears!

I look everywhere! I ask everyone! But no Adam! My child is missing!

I run outside into the parking lot. No Adam! I run down the street. I call his name! "Adam! Adam! Adam!"

Where is my child? There he is! He is standing and talking to a young woman.

The young woman shows me how she found out who Adam is, and where he lives.

"What is your mother's name?" she asks Adam.

"Mommy," says Adam.

"What is your father's name?" she asks him.

"Daddy," says Adam.

"What does your daddy call your mommy?" she asks.

"Mary," says Adam.

"What does your mommy call your daddy?"

"Paul," says Adam.

"And what is your address?" she asks.

Adam knows his address perfectly, right down to the apartment number!

Our second child is called Anne, after my mother. Anne is not as independent as Adam. When we go for walks in the forest, Anne goes a little way, and then she wants to be picked up. Meanwhile, Adam runs ahead. He is very athletic, like I was.

Getting outside the city is good for my children's health. In the summer, they stay at the little cottage where my husband's parents live. This cottage is just outside our city. It has a pond. One day, Anne and our third child, Andrew, see ducklings in the market.

"Oh, Mommy!" Anne exclaims. "Can we have ducklings for our pond? Please? They're so cute!"

"Please, please!" Andrew pleads. "Can we have ducklings?"

I buy two ducklings, one for each child. Anne holds her duckling very carefully, but Andrew keeps hugging his duckling and crooning, "My ducky! My ducky!"

Soon Andrew's duckling is dead. Poor little Andrew can't stop crying.

And Anne's duckling, who has been left all alone without a brother or a sister, is going, "Peep, peep, peep!"

So my husband says, "Mary, you must buy another duckling tomorrow when you go to the city. In fact, get two—one for Adam too. He is too proud to ask for such a babyish present, but he would enjoy a duckling too."

So the next morning, on my way to work, I stop at the market to buy two more ducklings.

Only one farmer is selling ducklings this morning, and he does not want to sell two ducklings. He has *twenty* ducklings to sell.

"All right," I sigh. "How much for *all* the ducklings?"

"One hundred zlotys," he says.

"That is robbery, but my Andrew is crying, so I'll take them," I say.

And I put twenty ducklings in my shopping basket and rush off to work.

All day long as I examine patients, twenty ducklings sit in a corner of my office. Twenty ducklings go, "Peep, peep, peep!"

When the last patient is gone, I take the ducklings to the cottage.

The ducklings thrive in their new home.

Anne's lonely duckling is happy. Andrew is happy. Adam is happy.

These ducklings soon grow up. Every day we have duck eggs for breakfast, duck eggs for our neighours, and duck eggs to sell at the market.

And this is how we manage when times are difficult. We sell duck eggs, and other produce, that we grow at the grandparents' cottage. Even though my husband is a teacher, and I am a doctor, we do not have much money. Under the communist system, educated people do not make as much money as they do in the capitalist system. A doctor often makes less money than her patients.

Part of our salary goes to saving for an apartment for each of our children. We have to save ten or even twenty years for an apartment. There are not enough places to live in Poland, because building takes so long. There are not enough materials. There is not enough money. Central planning and corruption make every enterprise slow and difficult.

Another part of our salary goes to the rebuilding of Poland. In proportion to its size and population, Poland was the most destroyed of any country during World War II. For a whole generation—over thirty years—we Poles pay to rebuild our country.

I am often tired because I am so busy. I work extra hours at the hospital, so I can become a specialist and earn more money to help the family. I also wash and iron the family's laundry. And I do the cooking, cleaning and shopping. Shopping is especially difficult. I must stand in line. I must wait and wait.

One day when Anne and Andrew are being very

naughty, I lose my temper and snap: "Go out into the world! See how you like it there! Otherwise, you'd better learn how to behave!"

Then I stamp off to continue with the washing, cooking, or whatever I am doing. I am so busy that I do not notice what Anne and Adam are doing. They take their toothbrushes and slip out the main door of the apartment. They descend the stairs and emerge into the open air.

They do not go far. They hover at the entrance to our building, trying to decide where to go.

Along come Paul and Adam back from school.

"Anne! Andrew!" Paul exclaims. "What are you doing here with your toothbrushes?"

"We were very naughty, and Mommy said we must go out into the world, but we don't know which way to go!"

Then Anne and Andrew begin to cry.

"Oh, no!" exclaims Paul. "You don't have to go out into the world. You come back to the apartment with Adam and me. You apologize to Mommy for being naughty. She will forgive you."

Anne and Andrew come back to the apartment. Of course I forgive them. I hug them both and kiss them. But Anne and Andrew go on crying for a long time. All evening they sniff. And so do I.

Eva

I feel horribly guilty. Naomi and Curtis were out together somewhere, and Joe and I went for a walk. We left Hanna with a new hospice volunteer, and a new nurse came. Apparently, this nurse gave Hanna an unprescribed pill to ease her pain.

The volunteer couldn't remember what the nurse said the pill was. She said that Hanna knew the pill was something she hadn't tried before and consented to take it.

By the time we got back, Hanna had slipped into a coma. The expression on her face was terrible— almost as though she were screaming. I think the pill was causing her to hallucinate.

I talked to Hanna as much as I could. I reassured her that, when the effects of the pill wore off, she would feel better. I am sure she heard me. I told her to move her feet if she heard me, and she did.

Hanna's facial expression is more relaxed now. Eight hours have passed, and another nurse has just been and gone. This nurse said that the pill the new nurse gave Hanna can indeed cause hallucinations in some people. She also said that Hanna no longer feels physical pain.

The nurse noticed that Hanna sometimes stops breathing momentarily. The end is near.

Joe

Sponsoring someone to come to Canada is complicated. I photocopied several pieces of identification—both Eva's and mine. I typed a formal letter inviting Mary's daughter to come to Canada for two months and stay with Eva. I went to City Hall to fill in approved forms and obtain proper certification. I obtained the name and address of the Canadian ambassador in Warsaw from the office of our federal member of parliament. Finally, I faxed everything to said ambassador. The process took most of a day.

I don't think anybody invited my dad's family to come to Canada from Holland back in the 1920s. They just came. Or did they? Must ask Aunt Helen.

Except for helping Eva, and chatting with Curtis, everything is pretty much the usual grind. I am glad the semester is almost over. I'm tired. Eva is exhausted.

"Don't be such a perfectionist," I tell her, but she says she can't sleep all night anyway, so she might as well work.

Hanna is near the end.

The boys enjoyed biking around the local wildlife park and drawing some of the animals. All with Curtis. Meanwhile, I took a leisurely walk with my cameras.

Curtis followed the park expedition with "a scary, gross, new movie" on video: *Godzilla*. This exciting entertainment was accompanied by a large pepperoni pizza and a gooey chocolate cake, both purchased for a bargain price at the store where Curtis works.

Meanwhile, I ate a bowl of oatmeal porridge and made up exam questions.

Godzilla was a hit with the boys, as were the pizza and cake. Never underestimate the rotten taste of the average, male child—my sons!

Week Thirteen

Naomi

Sunday, December 5, 1999

On Tuesday, Joe and I took Mary from the hospital to her landlady's house. Mary's landlady must like Mary a lot. She wants to cook meals for Mary and take them to her in her room when Mary has to stay in bed. She will do this for free, as long as we buy Mary's groceries.

I visit with Mary for an hour after school every day, before I go home to eat dinner and do my homework. Mom comes home earlier from work now.

Hanna is really close to death. She is in a sort of coma. The nurse told Mom that "hearing is the last sense to go," so we must be careful what we say around Hanna. Mom bursts into tears a lot. I don't know what to do for her.

Curtis borrowed Joe's truck and drove me to get some groceries for Mary. Mary insists on paying for her own groceries.

Sarah is going through another phase of not paying

much attention to me. Sarah's brother got arrested for pushing drugs, and Sarah herself is having problems with her boyfriend. Personally, I suspect Sarah is sleeping with her boyfriend. Even if that is true, I can't understand why she is avoiding me. Does she think I would criticize her? Maybe I would, but so what? Sarah says she's failing all her courses. Why did she give up on school?

Mary has a lot of doctor's appointments in the next few weeks. Joe or Curtis and I are going to drive Mary to these appointments.

Joe contacted the Canadian ambassador in Warsaw. He and Mom asked the ambassador to give Mary's daughter a temporary visa for Canada, and he agreed to do this. Joe says he'll drive me to the airport to pick up Anne. Mary's landlady says Anne can stay on a cot in Mary's room.

* * *

I've still got to do homework, of course. The history project is almost finished. Here is a quote from *The Breakup of the Soviet Union* by B. Harbor: "20 August 1968. Soviet and other Warsaw Pact tanks invade Czechoslovakia to force liberal leader Alexander Dubcek to back down on reform plan."

* * *

What Naomi's neighbour, an old Czechoslovakian woman, said when Naomi interviewed her:

Since 1968, I have not gone back to Czechoslovakia. My brother, who still lives in Prague, can sometimes get to Vienna, so we meet there. When Czechoslovakia was still communist, we could talk on the telephone between Canada and Czechoslovakia. We would hear a "click", and we would know someone was listening to our conversation. So we'd switch languages—maybe from Czech to German. Then there was another "click", and somebody else who spoke German was listening. So we switched languages again—maybe from German to French. Then there was another "click". What an incredible effort was used for spying on us!

* * *

What an old Polish woman, a friend of the Czechoslovakian woman, said when Naomi interviewed her in the Czechoslovakian woman's kitchen:

I never saw my sister again after World War II, until 1992 when I went back to Poland. I was in Canada. She was in Poland. We'd write letters, of course, but they always arrived months late and censored. There would be holes where the most innocent remarks were made. The post office spent most of its time spying on us, rather than trying to deliver letters on time. Anyway, I didn't want to send her too many letters. She could get in trouble just because she had a sister living in the West. We were always very careful.

* * *

Sarah phoned. She said she has quit her band, and she might quit school. I asked her why. She said, "Sorry, but I've got to go now." Then she hung up.

* * *

My history project is due in one week. Mr. Dunlop said I had to have more documentation from "authoritative written material", like books, newspapers and magazines. That is why I have been looking through a scrapbook Mom made for me when I was a kid. I don't want to go to the library. It is crowded with other students who are doing projects too. Mom cut out the following article seventeen years ago. I copied the article exactly. It was on the front page of the *Globe and Mail* on Monday, December 14, 1981. Here is how it begins:

Immediate Mass Strike Urged
Angry citizens take to the streets after Poland declares martial law

WARSAW—Poles reacted angrily and swiftly yesterday to the imposition of nation-wide martial law by the country's Communist authorities.

After a Military Council of National Salvation assumed power, police used water cannons to disperse angry crowds outside the Solidarity union's Warsaw headquarters and union activists distributed leaflets calling for an immediate general strike.

Troops, tanks, armored personnel vehicles and riot police took up positions in Poland's large cities and on main roads. In a nation-wide, overnight operation about 1,000 people were reported detained, although authorities refused to reveal the exact number.

* * *

I might also use another article from the scrapbook. It was in *Time* on January 4, 1982. Here are the headlines:

Man of the Year
He Dared to Hope
Poland's Lech Walesa led a crusade for freedom

In this *Time* magazine article, there is a picture of Lech Walesa that shows my father standing near him. I have looked at this picture many times. My mother used to show it to me whenever I asked about my father. I used to ask a lot when I was little.

Mom used to say that my father looked "tall, dark and homely". She said Dad looked like the CBC newsman Terry Milewski, "Except Milewski's better looking."

Recently Mom said my father is "probably paunchy and grey-haired now".

I said: "That's better than being bald like Joe."

But now I'm sorry I said that, because Joe is being really nice to Mary and Curtis.

The experience of looking at my father's face is always cold but gentle. It's like the snow flurries that began to drift down as I looked this time. If my father likes my history project, I'm not going to *ask* him if I can visit him some day. I'm just going to get on a plane, go to Warsaw and *pound* on his door until he opens it.

Curtis

School and work are tolerable.

Naomi is worried about her mother and her friend, Mary, as well as her history project.

Naomi's mother is grief-stricken about her sister.

Mary reminds me of a snow goose driven far from her flock in a storm, like in the Paul Gallico story that Dad gave me when I told him I wanted to be an artist. Mary's voice is quiet, but I hear a honk of distress in it.

Mary is a small woman. She looks more like a sparrow than a goose. It's her *soul* that makes me think of a snow goose.

Mom is staying off my case and getting her own life together. She told Steve to move out. She threatened to call the cops if he didn't. She told him she doesn't want to see him again, "until he stops boozing and being abusive." She's going to a stress counsellor her doctor recommended.

I spent last Sunday afternoon in the wildlife park. I biked around with Joe's kids, then I showed them how to draw beavers, porcupines, raccoons and black bears. Joe walked around by himself and took photos.

Joe says: "Don't order women around. Let them see they can depend on your inner and outer strength, if they need to. Gently guide them, if they ask for help."

Joe says I can use his truck whenever I need it.

Judo's great. The first thing you learn is how to break your falls by rolling. Then you learn how to get your opponent off balance. Then you learn how to throw him. My goal is to get a black belt within a year.

Mary

The Prostitute and the Pickles

My cousin knows some people in Gdansk on the Baltic coast. That is why she can invite me and my husband and children to go for a seaside holiday for the whole summer and stay for free in a vacant apartment. We take the streetcar every day to the beach, where the children make sandcastles and swim.

Next door to where we are staying, a poor widow lives with eight children. This widow had six children of her own. Then, when a prostitute died leaving two neglected, harum-scarum children, the poor widow adopted those children too.

The prostitute's children are difficult, disobedient and backwards. They even go to the bathroom in strange places like the hallway. But the poor widow treats them like her own. She gives them lots and lots of love.

This widow does not have enough money for proper food and clothes for her children.

"I know how you can earn money," I say to her.

"How?" she asks.

"Sell pickles at the seashore," I say. "There are hundreds of people at the seashore every day. I am sure they would buy something refreshing and inexpensive like pickles."

"Impossible!" she says.

"I'll help you," I say.

The next day, early in the morning, I go with the widow to the farmer's market. I lend her the money to buy a big basket of baby cucumbers, some salt, garlic, mustard seeds, horseradish and dill. Oh yes, and a nice, clean, new, wooden barrel. Then, after my husband takes the widow's children and our children to the seashore, the widow and I make pickles. We put our ingredients in the barrel. Then we cover the barrel and leave it in a dark place in the widow's apartment for five days.

When the pickles are ready, the widow fills a bucket with them, boards the street car, and travels to the last stop—the beach. She sells the whole pailful in fifteen minutes at three zlotys per pickle. Then she returns to her apartment for another pailful.

By the end of the day, all the pickles in the barrel are sold. Now the widow has enough money to pay me back. She can also buy more cucumbers, salt, garlic, mustard seeds, horseradish and dill. And four more barrels. Meanwhile, her children have played all day at the seashore with my children.

My husband and I watch over all the children, so the widow is free to work. We watch the children play games together. We talk to them. And soon the prostitute's children stop going to the bathroom in strange places and begin to act more normally.

Soon the widow is selling pickles every day. By the end of the summer, she has enough money to buy food and clothes for her children. She can even buy them books for school.

Capitalism can be good.

And you know what? Those backward children of the dead prostitute grow up to be wonderful adults. The girl becomes a jeweller, making beautiful rings and bracelets. The boy becomes an electrician. Because they are orphans, the government supplies them each with a free apartment when they grow up.

Communism can be good too.

Both of them always remember their adoptive mother on her birthday and name day, at Easter and at Christmas. They always give her a nice gift, a kiss and a hug.

My husband, children and I never forget the summer of our wonderful, seashore vacation.

Not many summers later, in 1980, the Solidarity Uprising begins in the Lenin Shipyards at Gdansk. The shipyards are not far from where the children made sandcastles and the widow sold pickles!

Solidarity is not led by the uneducated electrician, Lech Walesa. It is led by Pope John Paul II. Karol Wojtyla was a cardinal in Krakow and a professor of ethics in the Lublin Catholic University before he became Pope. Our Polish pope knows many languages. He has two doctorates. He is well educated.

When Pope John Paul II comes to Poland for his first visit in 1979, Polish people go in the millions to attend his masses and see him pass in the popemobile.

The state television tries to show that there are not that many people, but we know how many there are.

We follow John Paul II on his pilgrimage to our holiest places at Gniezno, Czestochowa, Krakow and Oswiecim. Oswiecim is where, at the notorious Nazi concentration camp known in German as "Auschwitz", a Polish priest, Maksymilian Maria Kolbe, gave his own life so another could live. Kolbe is a saint now.

It is the pope who first talks about "solidarity". Solidarity is not forced on us. Solidarity is not politics. It is truth.

Then martial law is declared in Poland, and ordinary life becomes more difficult than ever.

Now it is really war again.

Eva

For three days and nights she lay unconscious and seemingly oblivious to everything. She ate nothing. But then eating had been almost impossible for some time. She swallowed, however, when I tipped a sip of water over her dry lips.

Perhaps it was the Chopin waltz that aroused her.

"Come here," she said to me, only now she could not speak. She only gestured with her hand. Or did she? Perhaps I only imagined that she signalled.

I laid my head on her breast. On the breast that was not diseased. I put my arms around her gently.

Soon, there was a rattle and a last breath. Soon, the last pulse was throbbing in her throat like the heartbeat of a little bird.

Sunlight flooded the little room.

"Much sunshine!"

Joe

Hanna is gone.

A noble soul.

I wish I had known her better, but by the time she

came to Eva's, she was too weak for much interaction.

I felt that my job was to stay in the background, avoid intruding on her privacy and instead support Eva.

Why could our rich, smug, North American society not offer Hanna a decent place?

If there is a God, I hope He can forgive us.

Week Fourteen

Naomi

Sunday, December 12, 1999

Hanna died last Sunday morning at about 11 o'clock.

I have never seen a dead person before.

Mom was alone with Hanna when she died. I was playing a Chopin waltz on the piano in the living room.

Mom sat with Hanna's body for a while. Then Mom's English Canadian doctor came, pronounced Hanna dead and left. Then two men came from a funeral home and took the body away.

I was there.

"She looks as though she's had a hard time," said one of the funeral home men.

"Yes, she has," said Mom calmly.

The men put Hanna's body in a big bag. Then they carried the bag out the front door on a stretcher.

Mom went afterwards to the funeral home to visit the body. She walked over to the "home" by herself. She said she wanted to go alone.

Mom is taking three weeks off work—until after the New Year. She is exhausted. Luckily classes at the college are finished. Hanna waited to die at the most convenient time possible for Mom.

There isn't going to be a funeral, because Hanna didn't want one. Hanna is going to be cremated, as she requested. In the spring, Mom will take Hanna's ashes to a forest, as Hanna also requested.

I spent most of Sunday afternoon in my room alone. I lay on my bed thinking for a long time. Then I got up, went to my desk and wrote down my thoughts. Here they are.

Death is absence. Life is there, and then it is not.

What remains after death is spirit.

The world is often evil and dark, but one person's spirit can be a light for the whole world, a force for good.

Hanna tried to be a light for the world. Did she succeed? Sometimes what she did made my mother and me unhappy. She also made herself unhappy.

Yet she did good. She made the world a better place.

Despite her successes, grief overwhelmed Hanna for a while, taking away her hope. But then, after she came to our home, hope began to return.

True, she wanted euthanasia. But she didn't want to die because the world is too evil. She wanted to die because she could no longer live with dignity.

I did not understand Hanna very well. I still don't. She was a very different kind of person than I am. Still, I admire her. I also feel sorry for her. Maybe if Hanna had received the right kind of help, she could have got better.

I hope my friend Mary's cancer has not spread too far! I hope the doctors can save her!

I wish I knew how to pray.

* * *

The title of my history project is, "Mary's Story: An Example of How the Broad Forces of History Affect the Private Lives of Individuals." The title is Mr. Dunlop's idea. I am using quotes from Mary's stories—not *everything* she said. Then I am adding quotes from other people, as well as newspapers, magazines and books. I have a time chart at the beginning:

September 1939—Beginning of World War II: Mary is an innocent six-year-old who will see many terrible things that will make her want to be a doctor. Her family is quite religious.

1945—Beginning of Cold War: Mary's family starts over again, like they did after World War I.

1956—Soviet troops invade Hungary: Mary works as country doctor.

1968—Soviets invade Czechoslovakia: Mary is raising her children and practising medicine in a big city. It is difficult to make a living because she is not a communist.

1980—Solidarity Uprising begins: Mary's children are teenagers. Mary and her children, like most Poles, agree with Solidarity.

December 1981—Declaration of Martial Law: Life is hard and dangerous. Food is scarce; wages are low. Mary is widowed.

1989-91—Fall of communism in Eastern Europe: Mary's savings are gone. She has a poor salary and pension. She leaves for Canada and starts all over again to build a life.

1999—Experience with capitalism reveals problems with that system: Mary has been working as cleaner in Canada for four years full-time. She is reduced to part-time. She becomes ill.

Curtis

The life within Hanna was fading when I met her. She was like a fallen bird. She had hit the window of mankind's indifference.

Yet, Hanna looked at me lovingly. She smiled at me. "Your young artist is very nice," Hanna told Naomi.

Hanna said this as I stood beside Naomi. These were the only words she spoke in my presence. She said the words slowly and clearly in English, so I would understand.

Hanna thought that being an artist was an honorable career, not shameful. She felt me worthy of this honour.

I am grateful.

Mary

No Guns!

When the Solidarity movement is fighting for the freedom of Poland, it does not use guns. Instead, it uses the truth.

There are open-air performances where poetry is recited into loudspeakers. And people applaud because the poetry tells the truth about life. About how we are not free or equal. Communism is good in theory. It means equality for all. But communism is not good in practice. If you belong to the Polish United Workers' Party—that's what the communist party is called—you have a powerful position and an instant apartment. You have these things even though you do nothing. If you do not belong to the Party, you have nothing, even if you work hard all your life.

Corruption ruins any system—communist or capitalist.

People look out their darkened windows at night, and suddenly they see lights in other windows. The lights spell, "Solidarity!" Then the lights go out. Then they come on again in a different place.

When Solidarity is forbidden to meet or distribute information in Poland, it launches big balloons over the Baltic Sea. The balloons float to Poland, burst, and drop thousands of pamphlets telling everyone about the work of Solidarity.

Polish people are forbidden to have radios. They must give their radios to the police. But everybody still knows what is going on. Information travels quickly from one end of the country to the other by word of mouth.

Oh yes, after so many centuries of invasions, wars and insurrections, Poland knows how to fight! With no guns!

You have to use your wits. Take my son Adam. He's almost grown up now. He loves to tinker with mechanical things, just like my brother Johnny.

When a curfew is imposed, we are careful to be

indoors by ten p.m. But one day, when Adam visits a friend, he comes home late. Usually I am in bed by ten o'clock, but at fifteen minutes after the hour, I am so worried that I am fully dressed. I am pacing back and forth in the apartment.

Twenty minutes after the hour, twenty-five minutes… There he is!

Quick! Open the door! He's in!

He's breathing hard from running—dodging the police.

Adam hides his cap and jacket under the pillows on the couch. Then he lies down on the couch and pretends to be reading a magazine.

"If the police come to the door, tell them I've been here all evening," he says.

The police do come, and I do tell them this.

The police believe me and go away.

Adam is planning to study engineering. First, however, he must serve two years in the Polish army. I miss him. The more so because I am a widow. It's difficult to believe that Paul has been gone five years!

Paul was tired and preoccupied. He was not watching where he was walking. He was hit by a streetcar and killed instantly. Luckily, I was not on emergency duty when they brought him in. Without my brother to help me, I don't know what I would have done.

As for my other son, Andrew, who is also a teenager, he uses his wits too. Andrew is a born businessman. Officially, of course, free enterprise is not encouraged under communism, but Andrew can sell anything from jeans to nuts, so he makes a little money to help his family.

Andrew's secret is that he talks to everyone easily. He is very charming, so people want to do business with him.

One day when I am having even more difficulty than usual getting meat, I express my frustration to the children.

"The situation is impossible!" I declare. "How on earth am I supposed to feed my family?"

"What's the problem?" asks Andrew.

"We have no meat!" I answer. "In three hours I could not get meat. I looked everywhere."

"If you give me money," says Andrew, "I'll get you meat. Tell me what you want, and I'll get it in a few moments."

"Nonsense!" I snap. "Don't be a silly, boasting little boy!"

"Give me some money, and tell me what you want," Andrew repeats firmly, holding out his hand.

I do as he says.

Sure enough, Andrew is back in a few minutes with a big package full of stewing beef and sausage.

Andrew knows all the shopgirls. He chats with them often. He is very handsome, as well as charming, and they like him. For Andrew, there is meat right away!

This Christmas, we still miss Paul. Luckily, some relatives are visiting today. Uncle Johnny is here, as well as Grandpa and Grandma. And Adam has been given leave from the army for a few days.

Because of Solidarity unrest, the communist government has soldiers posted everywhere. There is a soldier on guard just outside our apartment building.

As Anne and I are preparing Christmas dinner, Anne looks out the window at the soldier.

"That soldier looks lonely all by himself in the snow," says Anne. "Adam says that the soldiers get tired of eating the same boiled *kasza* day in and day out. Why don't I go and hang a bag of food on the fence for that soldier?"

Anne does this. When the soldier opens the bag, he finds cabbage rolls, herring, poppy-seed cake and other good things. He gulps down everything like a starved dog.

Then, with his feet, he writes "Merry Christmas!" in the snow. Then he goes on guarding the apartment building, looking as serious as ever.

Popieluszko, a young priest in Warsaw, is killed the next year. The communists think he is preaching politics and helping Lech Walesa, but that's not so.

I heard Popieluszko preach once—not in Warsaw, but in our own parish. He did not mention politics. He behaved like a good priest. He only talked about religion.

Solidarity fights with no guns, but still the government has to kill someone. So it seems.

Young Popieluszko is visiting another parish outside Warsaw. He leads a mass in Bydgoszcz. Afterwards, when the church chauffeur is driving Popieluszko home, the car is ambushed. The chauffeur escapes into the forest, so he lives. But Popieluszko dies. His body is found a few days later, in a reservoir of water. His hands and feet are bound, and there is a rope around his neck.

Everyone knows that the communist government

murdered him. The government thinks that, once Popieluszko is gone, everyone will stop going to church.

Ha!

Of course, I myself always go to church on Sunday. Otherwise, with all I've been through, I'd have taken to drink long ago. But now everyone goes to church. People who have not been inside a church for years start going again!

One nurse, whose family lives in Bydgoszcz, tells us what is happening there. Outside the church where Popieluszko gave his last mass, people make a huge cross with candles.

The authorities claim that the candles are a fire hazard. This is a lie.

The authorities remove the candles.

People make another huge cross. This time with flowers.

The authorities remove the flowers.

But people replace the flowers.

Day after day, week after week, month after month, year after year, people keep placing flowers on that cross.

That's how to fight! With flowers!

Eva

Hanna decided on cremation. She did not want announcements of her death in the newspapers. She did not want a funeral. She did not want to be buried in the Catholic cemetery.

She did not want anything more to do with churches.

"I come from that tradition," she said, but said no more. I assume she meant that, for her, tradition had failed to keep up with the truth.

"Take me to the forest," she said. "Leave me there."

I arranged to meet the body in the plain wooden box when it arrived at the crematorium. While I waited, I inspected the huge oven, the sterile metal tables and trays. While I waited, I heard the remote, leafless trees calling out to the heavens in eery, distant keening.

It is the millions, I thought. *She is finally joining the millions who died at Auschwitz.*

I watched as the oven's powerful, jet-like flames began to burn the box.

Joe

I drove Eva to the crematorium to witness the arrival and burning of Hanna's body.

The crematorium is about fifteen kilometres from Mapleville in rolling farmland. Apparently, it is the only crematorium in the region. I'd never noticed it before. It's situated well back from the highway. From a distance, it looks like a modern, brick farmhouse.

Rest in peace, Hanna. You were an outstanding human being.

You suffered far more than I can ever know.

Hanna was a symbol of her martyred country. Who said, "Poland is the Christ of nations"? Winston Churchill?

The Poles suffered more than even the Dutch during World War II. Of course, I myself was not in

Holland during the war. I was a toddler in Canada.

Hanna was a woman of extraordinary courage and penetrating intelligence. As well, she had the moral authority of a saint.

I have never understood traditional, Catholic saintliness, but Hanna's saintliness transcended religious boundaries and communicated even to a struggling agnostic like me.

She was a hero.

Week Fifteen

Naomi

Sunday, December 19, 1999

A few days ago, Joe drove me to the airport to meet Mary's daughter. Anne said she would be holding up a white sign with red heart on it. The sign flopped over, so I almost didn't see it.

Anne, or "Anna" as she is called in Polish, is in her late twenties. She has two children. She's tall, thin, glamorous and blonde—like Sarah, only more mature and refined. She is sweet, gentle, caring and loving. She speaks little English, and I speak almost no Polish, so communicating is difficult. We use a lot of gestures, and we draw pictures.

Mary's operation is tomorrow.

I am thankful that Anne is here, because I have no idea how to take care of somebody after an operation.

Mom cleaned out Hanna's room. She really scrubbed it. She also organized the boxes of Hanna's papers that were stacked in the living room. Joe carried the boxes down to the basement and put them on shelves that he had made.

Mom says Mary can stay with us when she comes out of the hospital. Mary can stay in Hanna's room. Anne can also stay in that room. I'll stay in the basement room.

Mom says Mary can stay in our house for as long as she wants to. Mary can stay for free while she is recovering. Anne can stay for free until she goes back to Poland in February. When Mary is better, she can work as a housekeeper for Mom and Joe, if she wants to.

The head of the nursing team that took care of Hanna came to "say goodbye" and pack up the medical equipment the team left behind. She sent Hanna's hospital bed back to the medical-supplies place. She said that Mary would be fine on an ordinary bed like the one we had stored in our basement. Curtis and Joe carried that bed upstairs and put it in Mary's room.

I spend as much time as possible with Anne. Curtis says he'll drive Anne and me anywhere we need to go, as long as Joe isn't using his truck.

Curtis has been more of a friend to me than Sarah has. I thought boys were gods, not friends. I can talk to Curtis about almost anything. He is a good listener, as well as a good observer.

*   *   *

Sarah phoned a few minutes ago. She is *pregnant*, and her brother is in *jail!* Her parents are furious with both her and her brother.

Her father says Sarah should have an abortion, but her mother says abortion is a sin. Sarah hasn't decided what to do. If she keeps her baby, she loses her boyfriend, and she can't go to Paris, or New York, or anywhere.

Actually, Sarah may have lost her boyfriend already. He took off when she told him she was pregnant. He left town, and his roomates don't think he is coming back.

I told her that I won't desert her. I also promised that I would help her more when I am not so busy with schoolwork and worried about Mary.

Then Sarah said she wanted to kill herself.

I got angry and said that she was just being melodramatic. I also said that she ought to consider other people besides herself. Then I hung up.

After I hung up, I felt bad about what I had said. So I phoned Sarah back and told her she ought to phone the Mental Health Crisis Line, or talk to a guidance counsellor at school, or see her family doctor. I also told her that she can call me any time if she feels depressed. I also told her for the first time that my parents never married, and that I was illegitimate.

"Having a baby when you're single is not the end of the world," I said. "It's bad, but not terminal."

Sarah appreciated my saying this. I could tell because she was more quiet afterwards. She didn't sound so hysterical.

*   *   *

I love Curtis.

I guess Mom loves Joe the way I love Curtis. I know Mom wants to marry Joe, even though she thinks marriage is old-fashioned. I could tell by the way she told me that he asked her.

* * *

I handed in my history project a little early. It wasn't as perfect as I wanted it to be, but I couldn't work on it any more. I'm glad I did so much work for my history project and English journal before Mary got sick. The journal is almost finished. Now I just have to concentrate on passing my biology exam on Tuesday.

Curtis is good at biology, especially diagrams of course.

The grocery store where Curtis works says I can start being a cashier there immediately, but I'm going to wait until after the New Year. I have enough stress right now without trying to learn how to do a new job.

I never heard anything from the Rec Plex director. Neither did Mary.

I hope Grandma is enjoying Hawaii. She deserves some happiness.

* * *

I hope you don't mind, but now I'm going to fill in the rest of this week's journal entry with some interesting facts that I learned while doing my history project. Here is what *The Breakup of the Soviet Union* said about the collapse of Soviet communism: "In a very brief period between 1989 and 1990, communist regimes in Poland, East Germany, Czechoslovakia, Hungary and Romania were swept away in popular protests, and this time the Soviets did not intervene to save them."

*   *   *

Mom gave me the following, amazing quotation from a new book that Joe gave her. The book is called *Witness to Hope*. It is by George Weigel. It is a biography of Pope John Paul II. Here is the quote: "The Solidarity revolution, unique among all the revolutionary upheavals of modernity, killed precisely no one."

*   *   *

Joe gave me the following helpful quote from himself: "In some respects, the Polish Solidarity Uprising was the greatest of the four great passive-resistance movements of the second half of the twentieth century. I mean the protest movements led by Mahatma Gandhi in India, Martin Luther King Junior in the United States, Pope John Paul II in Poland and Nelson Mandela in South Africa. It was miraculous that the Polish Solidarity movement defeated the massively-armed Soviet empire through peaceful protest alone—that it killed no one."

Curtis

Mr. Speers framed "The Fallen Bird" drawing for me and entered it in a juried competition at the college. It won first prize.

A reporter interviewed me and took photos of me and the drawing. The article will be published in a couple of weeks. The judges said that I was competing against some senior college students with much more "formal training."

Naomi was incredibly impressed with me. So was I. So was Dad. Even Mom was impressed!

Mr. Speers said I can probably get a scholarship for art college now, as long as my *marks* are good.

Some new guys at the grocery store are fairly cool. They're a little older than me and already in second-year at the college. Kevin's in Environmental, and Brian's in Electronics. Brian hasn't had Eva for a teacher, but he says she's supposed to be tough. Kevin and Brian are old friends from North Bay. They do a lot of camping up there together. They said I could go with them some time.

No time to write more.

King Wolf needs marks to get out of his cage and into the forest.

Mary

Grandma! Grandma!

In the middle of the night, when I return from an emergency case at the hospital, I lift my infant grandson Stephen out of his crib and take him to the potty. Why not? My daughter-in-law needs her sleep. She is tired from chasing her little son all day long.

I lie awake thinking about things. Stephen is my third grandchild. Already he is two years old. Andrew is a business man. He travels back and forth to Germany constantly, so his wife and child need my help. My poor daughter-in-law! I'm no replacement for her handsome, dashing Andrew! Good thing he'll be home soon.

Adam and Anne are also married. They each have

one child. Adam is living in my brother's old apartment, because my brother is in Canada. Meanwhile, Anne and her husband are staying with my mother-in-law, now a widow as well as a great-grandmother. Adam is an engineer, and Anne is a nurse. They're very busy these days, struggling hard to make ends meet. I'd love to retire, but how can I? When communism fell, I started from zero again. My savings are gone.

Solidarity won freedom, but not prosperity.

Doctors' salaries are worse than ever. And if I retire, my pension will be too small to live on. My Polish pension would be the equivalent of about 200 Canadian dollars a month. How could I pay for food, clothes, telephone, heat, light, water and gas? The goods are in the shops now, but they're expensive. Besides, I want to help my children.

In my spare time, I knit mittens, hats, scarves and sweaters. I also sew everything from jackets, to dresses, to jeans.

Adam has a very good job, but his family is crowded into one single bachelor's apartment: two adults and one child in one small room. Anne's husband has a university degree. He is trained to be a teacher like Paul was, but he's trying to start a business. He thinks he can make much more money by selling flowers than by giving history lessons. He is probably right.

Should I give up medicine and go help Anne's husband with his business? No, they don't need Grandma as well as Great-grandma. Should I work as a doctor in some African country? No, too hot. I don't like heat.

What about Canada? There is only my brother to invite me. My sister Agnes is dead, and so is her husband. I can't impose on Agnes's grown children. I don't know them. I can't ask them to pay my airfare, then feed and house me until I establish myself.

Oh. The phone is ringing! What time is it? Five o'clock in the morning? I must have fallen asleep. I was dreaming that my oldest grandson, Michael, was very tiny—just a speck.

"Hello?"

"Mom? It's Adam. I knew you'd be getting up to go to work now."

"What's wrong, dear?"

"It's Michael. He's very ill. I'm afraid for him. He's been in the hospital for a week. First he had mumps. Now they think he has meningitis. They called a few moments ago. They said they don't know whether he is going to live....I'm so afraid."

"Goodness! I was dreaming about Michael just now. Don't worry, dear. That hospital near you is excellent. I know those doctors well. He'll receive the best care possible. You must pray, and I'll pray too. You know what?"

"What?"

"My mother had a terrible case of mumps when I was a child. The side of her neck was as big as a bunch of bananas. She was unconscious. She didn't recognize us. The doctor wrote out a prescription, but he told us that she probably wouldn't live.

"After the doctor left, an old neighbour woman dropped by to see how things were. She found us children crying and my father in despair.

191

"'Listen to me,' said the neighbour woman. 'Here's an old folk remedy that the young doctor probably doesn't know. Take flax seeds, make a poultice, and put it in a linen cloth. Heat the poultice in the oven, and put it on the swelling on your wife's neck. When the poultice cools down, heat it in the oven again, and put it on your wife's neck again. Keep doing this until the swelling goes down.'

"'I'll try anything,' said my father. 'Johnny, you get some flax seeds from the barn. Elizabeth, you find a clean linen cloth. Mary, you run to the apothecary shop. Get this prescription filled. Cut through the cemetery, so you'll get back sooner.'

"I bolted out the door and sprinted down the street at top speed. It was night. I had never before entered the cemetery in the dark. I was terrified! But I passed those scary graves without stopping, and I got home with my mother's medicine in record time.

"My father gave my mother the doctor's medicine, then he followed the neighbour's instructions carefully. In a few hours, the swelling on my mother's neck had gone down. She opened her eyes and recognized us.

"'Why am I here in bed?' she asked. Then she fell asleep. The next day she was much better, although still very weak."

"Thanks, Mom," says Adam.

"For what?" I ask.

"For the story," says Adam.

That afternoon I phone Adam. Michael is getting better!

That evening my brother phones me. He asks me to

come to Canada. His wife is very ill, and he needs help to take care of her.

I say I'll come right away.

Eva

As Hanna and I were leaving the Auschwitz Museum twenty years ago, I noticed something white and fluffy and cottony floating in the hot, still air. This fluff was carrying seeds from the poplar trees. I thought of this fluff as millions of torn souls, clumped together.

When I found Hanna lying paralyzed and dying of cancer six months ago in her room in Montreal, this same fluff was in the air. It clung to the poplar trees outside her window. It clumped on the windowsill of her little rented room. It entered the room.

Hanna too was little more than a skeleton—a boney ruin like the people in the photographs at the museum. But it was by the way she lived that I knew for certain that she was one of the Auschwitz millions, even though she had miraculously escaped death there. She was at one with them.

Always she lived for others. Always she gave. Always she fought for what she believed was right. She fought fiercely for truth, for justice, for humanity.

She never relented, even as she lay dying. I knew she was one of them. One with them. One with the millions.

I knew this. But she never said that this was so.

"What was your purpose in life?" I asked her.

"To pass a message," she replied.

*   *   *

Here is a poem Hanna wrote for one of her adopted sons. I have just translated it from French. I never knew Hanna to write a poem, so I was surprised to find this.

Our Reality According to Me

You told me
"I am not God"
and I know this well.
You are Man.
I have entered
into an imaginary place to live in your landscape
in order to be created anew
and inside out.
That is to say
it is necessary
to find the sensation of tenderness again.
You are how you are—
you, for whom the clouds and birds
sing.

I am
an awkward, crippled witch full of complex simplicity.
I climb the stairs to find my life
enclosed
in your hand.
I don't know why
but it is there.
My life

your life
password
of the magic square of____Avenue
by way of the fourth dimension
to the fifth
all equally important.
The little cat Mitsou
plays with the light.
The sun lingers beyond the window.
You tell me
"I don't need you."
You gave me
even so
the most beautiful gift
important and difficult—
You.

It is difficult to live in emptiness.
It is difficult to live against the times,
against all the hostile forces.
But you know
I am going to try to do the impossible,
and I do not accept defeat.
And
so
accept
by kindness
my failures
which
wound you and set you
against me.

In searching for lost sense,
in searching for lost times,
at war against all absurdity
—all false evidence—
I take you
as clear light, as faint light,
as light
for the way
to I don't know where.

I should like to give something—
a drop of rain
that is not too acid
without any importance
which by chance
reflects the universe
—a home
for wanderers
and birds,
a refuge
for renewal.

Joe

After I picked up Mary's daughter at the airport and
brought her to Eva's, Naomi hugged me and thanked
me!

The semester is over. Eva needs to rest and grieve.
I am holidaying with the boys.

I took the boys skiing for several days. I also took
them to Toronto several times. We did the Ontario
Science Centre and the Royal Ontario Museum. We

let Curtis get on with passing his exams, working at the store and courting Naomi.

Hanna has taught me, among other things, that life's too short to do what you don't believe in.

I will retire from teaching as soon as possible.

I will earn a living in a way that does not exhaust me.

I will allow myself to be directed from within.

Week Sixteen

Naomi

Sunday, December 26, 1999

In Grandma's postcard from Hawaii, the water is blue, the palm fronds are green, and the sand is pinkish. In Mapleville today, the sky is grey, the tree trunks are black, and the snow is white. This afternoon, Mary wanted to sleep, so Joe, Mom, Anne and I went for a walk in the big nature park outside Mapleville. Curtis didn't come because he is in Windsor visiting his grandparents.

Anne loves wild animals almost as much as Curtis does. I'm glad I explored this park today, because now I will be able to talk with Curtis about something that interests him.

Mary still has some pain, and she is weak from her operation, but she is very happy to have Anne with her.

Anne spent all day every day at the hospital while Mary was there. I only went after school. Before and after the operation, Mary's dark-grey eyes kept locking on my eyes or Anne's. After the operation, as

Anne and I stood on either side of Mary's bed in Intensive Care, Mary held our hands—one hand of each of us. Mary was grateful to be alive. Anne and I were like chains holding her to life.

Anne and Mary spend a lot of time talking quietly in Mary's room. Mom and I try to give them as much privacy and space as possible, and they do the same for us.

When we got back from our walk in the nature park, Mom went to her room, Anne went to hers, and Joe went home. I went to my room too. I lay down to think about everything, and I almost fell asleep. Suddenly some music for "The Blind Man's Song" started to play in my semi-unconscious mind.

As the darkness outside deepened, the music got louder and clearer. I went upstairs to the living room to try out the chords quietly on the piano and scribble them down on paper. Soon the whole piece was finished.

Then I sat on the couch for a while looking at our tiny Christmas tree. Mom and I don't believe in chopping down live trees to make temporary decorations, so we haul out the same little plastic tree every year. This year, the tree is on top of the book shelf in the livingroom. Hanging on the wall beside the tree is the sad but lovely "Fallen Bird" picture that Curtis won a prize for. Curtis gave me the picture for Christmas. I was thrilled.

I gave Curtis a big box of oil paints. He likes my present a lot.

I felt peaceful. Although Hanna died so tragically and so recently, my life seemed beautiful.

* * *

Mom really likes Mary and Anne. She says helping them helps her feel "slightly less devastated" about Hanna.

Joe and Curtis moved Mary's stuff to our house in Joe's truck.

Mary lives farther from the Catholic church now, but a priest will come to our house once a week to give Mary communion and hear her confessions.

Anne has to help Mary a lot. For example, Anne often brings little meals to Mary on a tray, so Mary can eat in bed.

Anne brought lots of photos of Mary's grandchildren. Mary looks at the photos over and over again.

The doctors think they caught Mary's cancer early enough, so it won't come back. Mary has to take lots of pills, though. She also has to eat a special diet, rest and see the surgeon every few months for a check-up. She won't be able to walk to church for a long time yet. But eventually she will be able to live more or less normally, as long as she is careful.

Mary can't go back to working full time, however, because that would be too hard for her physically and psychologically.

Mary is going to sew clothes for Mom and me, as well as for her grandchildren. Already Mary is planning to turn our backyard into a magnificent vegetable garden. Our front yard will be a lovely flower garden.

* * *

Curtis is talented, intelligent, sincere and funny. Also handsome and sexy.

I'm doing really well in English so far. (Thanks, Mrs. H.) I got a "B" in biology and an "A" on my history project. Mr. Dunlop wrote that I had "organized my material well."

Maybe I am going to be a doctor or a nurse, if I don't want to have a clothing boutique. Mom says my great-grandmother was studying to be a doctor when she dropped out of university to get married. She says I have other relatives who were doctors too. Actually, she says, I am becoming like one of them: Dr. Zosia.

Mom met Dr. Zosia in Poland twenty years ago, when Dr. Zosia was a very old lady. Mom says Dr. Zosia was a mentor for Mary. What a coincidence that I met Mary!

I sent a copy of my project to my father.

Curtis

I noticed a young, red-tailed hawk on a leafless tree branch beside the highway as Mom and I were driving back from Windsor after visiting her family for a few days.

Mom's older sister, Aunt Edith, says Mom should forget Steve completely and find another man. Grandma says Mom should start going to church again, do good deeds, and forget about men. Gramp doesn't say much, except "Hmph."

They all agree I did "real good" this term. They sincerely hope I "keep on learnin' and stay outta trubble."

I spent most of the visit in Gramp's workshop, doing a painting of glaucous and Iceland gulls against the background of a lake freighter docked on the Detroit River. Naomi gave me a great set of oil paints for Christmas.

Aunt Edith and Grandma said the painting was "real nice", almost as good as "wun-a-them-paint-by-numbers-pitchers". Gramp said, "Hmph."

Mom and I talked a lot during the drive back from Windsor. We laughed about the stuff her family said, but we also sort of agreed with them. They've got a lot of common sense.

I moved back in with Mom. She needs someone to shovel her snow this winter. Steve is definitely out of her life. I'll still visit Joe. We're good friends now.

Had a long talk with Dad on the phone. He's moved back to Edmonton, and he'll have more time now for our long-distance calls and summer visits.

Naomi and I can go out to Edmonton together next summer.

She will drag me to the West Edmonton Mall for shopping, and I will drag her to Elk Island National Park for sketching.

I made sketches of the caged timber wolves at the local wildlife park, and now I'm doing an oil painting of a big male wolf leading his pack through the primeval forest at dawn.

You can tell the leader is the strongest, the fastest and the smartest.

His mate is also strong, fast and smart.

She is alluring.

Woo-oo!

Mary

Canada

I had many years of experience in my own country as a doctor, a specialist. I even received awards for my work. But in Canada I could not find a respectable, paying job.

I stayed with my brother for two years, keeping house and caring for his sick wife. Then, after his wife died, I stayed with my brother for another year. Then I got my Landed Immigrant papers, took English lessons and looked for a paying job.

I could find nothing better than cleaning. I would not mind doing this job, if I were not highly educated, and if people treated me with respect.

Here in Canada, however, people often seem to think cleaners are not worthy of respect. They write with lipstick on the mirror. They spill pop on new rugs. They throw sticky garbage on the floor. They stuff paper towels in the toilet.

I am shocked by the casual vandalism and waste here in Canada. The director of the Recreation Centre, one of the places I worked, talked about saving money. But he did nothing about reducing the graffiti and garbage.

What a terrible waste of my talents, education and experience! Why couldn't someone have given me some little job related to medicine? I didn't need perfect English to be an assistant in a hospital.

If one of my children could have joined me, it wouldn't have been so bad. But the Canadian government wouldn't let even one of them immigrate. The government felt that I did not have enough money to sponsor a single grown child.

My child and I would have worked together. We would have found a way to manage in Canada without taking handouts.

It's too bad I didn't have enough money to go to school in Canada and requalify in my profession. My brother ate stale buns and lived in an unheated room while he requalified for engineering. And he wasn't so young then either.

The old fellow who owned the house where I rented a room was always complaining about foreigners coming here and taking away jobs from Canadians. I've never yet met any Canadian who wanted the jobs I did. Evenings, weekends, holidays—scrubbing toilets, sinks, floors. Usually all by myself.

Look at my red, swollen hands! My bulging knuckles! Those big, industrial metal buckets must weigh fifteen kilograms when they're full of water. Some days, I couldn't believe I could lift them.

I myself weigh only fifty kilograms!

"You're as skinny as a beanpole!" the old fellow said where I rented a room.

"You look like a pregnant cow!" I said to him.

He was angry, but his wife and I laughed. They were not so bad, the old couple. They were kind. Certainly, I preferred to live with *them* rather than with drunkards in a rooming house.

When I first left my brother's home in the country, I lived in a rooming house in Mapleville. The owner of the house was well off, but he never cleaned the place. The hallways smelled of urine. Many of the tenants drank. One of them came after me with a knife as I returned from work.

"Do you love me?" he asked, waving the knife. "Do you love me?"

"Oh, yes," I said, "I love you very much!"

Then I jumped inside my room, shut the door and locked it. The next day I phoned my brother and told him what had happened.

My brother came as quickly as he could. He helped me find this other place with the old couple. I was safe with them, and I had companionship.

I am shocked by how many people in Canada suffer from untreated psychiatric problems. I see many such problems here, even among young children.

This is a very harsh society, a frontier society—the "Wild West".

If there were a war here, the entire society would need psychiatric care.

Eva

In the spring, I shall scatter the purified remains of Hanna's bones deep in the forest in a beautiful, lofty place. The remains are tiny, crystalline boulders. Seeds.

Joe

I shared a subdued Christmas dinner with Eva, Naomi, Mary and Anne. No festivities or extras, due to Hanna's death being so recent.

Eva has been too close to despair for too long. She

has been blocking out her feelings with her overachiever activities. Mary says I should try to get Eva outdoors as much as possible. Fresh air and exercise. Fine with me.

Curtis's father did not come through with money for a car. The big California deal fell through. Curtis does not seem to mind. He is glad his father has more time to talk now. Curtis has good values.

Curtis has moved back in with his mother for the winter. She seems more reasonable now.

Curtis and I will still see each other, of course. I enjoy our conversations. He is a thinker. And of course we share an interest in the visual arts. We didn't visit the Toronto art galleries together, as we planned, but one day we will.

Before Christmas, Curtis caught a bus, went down to Toronto and bought me a very decent weather vane and mercury barometer as Christmas gifts from him and Naomi.

Eva gave me a hydrometer, so I'm all set up.

Looking forward to a blissful week of weather watching and puttering in the dark room.

Week Seventeen

Naomi

Friday, December 31, 1999

Yesterday we had a "memorial celebration" for Hanna in the living room of our house. Mom said it wasn't a funeral. It was an "unscripted, private gathering".

Mary and Anne just listened. Mom read some poems she found among Hanna's papers. I read the words I wrote after Hanna died. Joe and Curtis read some comments they had written about Hanna. Finally, we all listened to a performance of music called "Symphony of Sorrowful Songs", created in the 1970s by a Polish composer called Henryk Gorecki. Mary had told Joe about this symphony, so he bought a tape of it in Toronto.

Everything that everyone read was charged with emotion. I was amazed by how deeply everyone had been affected by Hanna, even though Hanna was mostly just a silent and invisible presence in the house for the past four months.

The "Symphony of Sorrowful Songs" is stunning. It is for instruments and human voices. I have never heard anything so original, pure, simple and powerful. Like prayer. Like a universal light radiating out of enormous and terrible darkness.

Joe found some notes about the symphony on the Internet. He read them to us before he started the tape. The notes said that the symphony belongs to a type of music called "Spiritual Minimalism", and that it "commemorates the holocaust of Auschwitz". The symphony is also about the "central source of poetic power" and the "theme of motherhood".

We were all silent for a long time after the music stopped. Then we slowly began to talk.

We realized that we have all been keeping diaries, and that we have been telling many things to the diaries instead of to each other. When I was talking about my diary, I mentioned "The Blind Man's Song". I even sang them the song, accompanying myself on the piano. Everyone said the song was "wonderful." Joe said that I should be "composing music as well as joining a choir."

* * *

We're not having a party for New Year's Eve. Anne and Mary are staying home and phoning their family in Poland. Joe, Curtis, Mom and I are having dinner together at Joe's place. (Joe and Curtis are cooking dinner for us and washing the dishes afterwards!) Then Joe and Mom are watching the millenium celebrations around the world on Joe's TV. Joe is going to tape all the celebrations, so Anne and Mary can see them later if they want to. Mary especially wants to see the Polish pope addressing the world from a balcony at the Vatican.

Curtis and I are going downtown to watch the free entertainment at Mapleville City Hall. We'll take in all the acts—the jugglers, singers, fireworks, etc. If there's a group of singers I like, or maybe a choir, I'm going to try to join it next year. We'll also skate on the rink outside City Hall. We'll have fun.

* * *

This morning while I was tidying my room, I started to feel a new song coming. I wrote down the words quickly. Then I started to think about the music. The music wouldn't come right away, so I am leaving that part for another day. Here are the words.

The Voices Blend

The voices blend
as we few send
our love
to the whole wide world.

We sing together,
we live together,
we love one other.
Yes we do.

Sweet harmony,
we call on thee
to ease the world's struggles
and pain.

Gentle love
shining above
come down
and show us the way.

* * *

Mom came down to my room not long after I wrote the above. She sat on my bed and asked me how I liked the "celebration" for Hanna. I told her I liked it a lot. I knew that she already knew this, and that she just wanted to talk.

"I want you to know that, even when I am very busy, I love you and think about you," Mom said. "Hanna once told me that the people you meet are the most important thing in life, and she was right. *You* are the most important thing in my life."

"I know how important Joe is to you," I said. "And I think you should marry him. I know you want to."

"It's too soon," Mom said.

"Wait until summer, then," I said. "Get married and then go trucking with Joe for a few months. I won't mind. I like Joe. He can never be my father, but he is my friend. And in the summer I'll be with Grandma and Curtis. You have to *enjoy* life. You take things too seriously. Not that you shouldn't be serious about the death of your sister.... "

"I'm still waking up frequently at night," Mom said. "I have felt Hanna's spirit standing beside my bed several times."

"I felt the presence of Hanna's spirit during our memorial celebration," I said.

Mom nodded but couldn't speak.

"Do you think Hanna is glad that Mary is here?" I asked.

"Yes. Very glad. She knows that Mary will take good care of us," Mom said. "She's already taking good care of us. There is a miracle in each of her stories!"

Then Mom looked at the framed poem on my wall: "Song for Naomi".

"I am upset that your 'Blind Man's Song' is so sad," said Mom. "It's very well done, of course. But it's very sad. Very...*negative*."

"Lots of people have sadness inside them at certain times of their life," I said. "That's normal. Curtis's drawing of the fallen bird is sad, but he's not depressed all the time. He's positive and creative. He just felt sympathy for the bird. And gratitude for what the bird had brought him. As for me, I was writing a new song today. A positive song. It isn't finished yet."

"Have I been a terrible mother?" Mom blurted suddenly.

"No," I said, feeling sort of embarrassed. "You've been working incredibly hard, plus you've had a lot of stress. The head nurse said you coped remarkably well. Remember?"

"Yes," said Mom. "That nurse was especially nice. After Hanna died, when she came to pick up the nursing equipment, she hugged me. I met another one of the nurses downtown a few days ago. She hugged me too."

"Well, there you go," I said. "They must approve of you."

"Do you think so?" said Mom. "Or are they just trying to comfort me?"

"Probably they approve of you, *and* they are trying to comfort you," I said, and I hugged her too. I gave her a great big hug.

As I held her, Mom started crying, so I started crying too.

We cried for a long time.

We also held each other for a long time, and rocked gently back and forth.

"So many tears," said Mom finally, grabbing a tissue from the box beside my bed, wiping her eyes and blowing her nose.

"So many drops of rain," I said, taking a tissue for myself and doing the same.

"'A drop of rain...that is not too acid...without any importance,'" began Mom.

"'Which by chance...reflects the universe,'" I finished.

We smiled shyly at each other.

Curtis

The private celebration that Naomi's family held for her aunt impressed me. It was unique. It was emotional, but not hysterical. The music Joe brought expressed hope. It also dealt with the problem of evil. To me, the music said that evil can and must be overcome.

In my painting of the wolf pack in the primeval forest at dawn, I don't include the dimension of evil, because man is not present. I think that in identifying with nature I have been shunning the evil I perceived in mankind.

One must fight evil, not flee it.

One must fight evil with good.

Luckily for me, art is good.

Mark

Warsaw, December 31, 1999

Dear Naomi,

Thank you for sending me your history project. I have read it with interest.

I apologize for not writing you before today. Please allow me to tell you a little about myself.

The struggle of the Solidarity movement to liberate Poland from the Soviet regime occupied me fully until about 1995, when Lech Walesa was largely discredited as a leader. During all those years, I was working as a translator for Solidarity.

In effect, I was working for the liberation of my country.

Today I earn a very good living by translating American books into Polish, or dubbing American films and television programs.

Let me also tell you a little about my family.

My father, B.I. Janasiewicz (1909-1982), was a journalist of some distinction. Unfortunately, my father felt he had to compromise his integrity to keep his family fed.

Initially my father joined the communist party because he believed in the party's goals. Subsequently he became disillusioned with party corruption. But he could not withdraw from the party without losing his power and influence.

My mother, born Irena Warszawska (1916-1981), was also a journalist before the war. In the postwar period, however, she stayed at home and devoted herself to the gentler pursuit of translating literary texts from French into Polish.

She also indulged in the hopefully pleasant task of caring for my father and me, her second and only surviving son.

My parents fell in love when my father's Catholic family hid my Jewish mother in their apartment during the war, saving her life. My parents had their first son in 1943, not long before the Ghetto Uprising. That son died during the war. I was born in 1957.

Naomi, perhaps you can be proud of me. I am at least a man who, for fifteen years in the prime of his life, followed his conscience and tried to change the world for the better.

I am also a man who now, in mid-life, would like to try to make amends for wrongs he committed long ago.

Perhaps it is not too late for you and me to become acquainted. What do you say? Can you forgive me? Are you willing?

I send you and your mother my best wishes.

Yours truly,

Mark Janasiewicz

Eva

This evening I am going to accept Joe's proposal of marriage. Naomi thinks I should. Time stopped when Hanna became ill. Soon time must begin again.

Joe

It is the eve of a new year, new century, and new millenium.

I hope the human race has learned from the mistakes of the past.

I hope I have too.

Heather Kirk has written newspaper and magazine articles, radio scripts, poetry and fiction. She has also taught for many years at universities and colleges.

Heather grew up in Oakville, Ontario, and studied English literature at Dalhousie University in Halifax, the University of Toronto and York University. She now lives with her husband and dog in Barrie, Ontario.

Heather has been interested in Eastern Europe and the Soviet Union since she was a teenager. She lived and worked in Poland between 1977 and 1979, and she has Polish friends still today. Poland has informed and inspired the writing of both the novels which she has published with Napoleon, *Warsaw Spring* and *A Drop of Rain*.